Death Benefits

SARAH N. HARVEY

Death Benefits

ORCA BOOK PUBLISHERS

Library and Archives Canada Cataloguing in Publication

Harvey, Sarah N., 1950-
Death benefits / written by Sarah N. Harvey.

Issued also in an electronic format.
ISBN 978-1-55469-226-2

I. Title.
PS8615.A764D42 2010   JC813'.6   C2010-903589-5

First published in the United States, 2010
Library of Congress Control Number: 2010929078

Mixed Sources
Cert no. SW-COC-001271
© 1996 FSC
FSC

*Orca Book Publishers is dedicated to preserving the environment and has printed
this book on paper certified by the Forest Stewardship Council.*

Summary: Royce is pressed into service as caregiver for his ninety-five-year-old
grandfather and gradually comes to appreciate the cantankerous old man.

Orca Book Publishers gratefully acknowledges the support for its publishing
programs provided by the following agencies: the Government of Canada through
the Canada Book Fund and the Canada Council for the Arts, and the Province of British
Columbia through the BC Arts Council and the Book Publishing Tax Credit.

Design by Teresa Bubela
Typesetting by Nadja Penaluna
Front cover image © Zoomstock/Masterfile
Back cover image by Dreamstime

ORCA BOOK PUBLISHERS
PO Box 5626, Stn. B
Victoria, BC Canada
V8R 6S4

ORCA BOOK PUBLISHERS
PO Box 468
CUSTER, WA USA
98240-0468

www.orcabook.com
Printed and bound in Canada.

13 12 11 10 • 4 3 2 1

For Lynne

One

"I can't take it anymore."

My mom is on the phone in the kitchen. I think she is crying. Or else her allergies are acting up again. Either way, she sounds miserable. She blows her nose vigorously as she listens to whoever's on the other end. I stop halfway up the stairs from the basement. I could easily slip back down to my room or sneak out the basement door, but something in her voice—desperation tinged with anger, muddied by snot—keeps me on the fourth stair from the top. That and the fact that she's obviously talking about me. Again.

"He's impossible, Marta," she says. "Absolutely impossible. Doesn't have any friends. Sleeps all day. Watches TV all night. Never showers. Refuses to cut his hair. Pushes his dirty dishes under the bed or stuffs them in drawers with his dirty underwear. I'm at my wits' end."

I want to leap into the kitchen and say, "Hey! It's only two o'clock. I'm up. I've had a shower. I'm dressed. And I never put dirty things—dishes or underwear—in drawers. I leave them on the floor. And when were you in my room anyway?" I have standards. Low ones, but still. She shouldn't be talking shit about me. It's true I haven't cut my hair for three years, but I wash it every couple of days. It's very fine and super straight, just like Mom's. You'd think she'd be a bit more sympathetic. And now she's complaining to Marta, who's probably not surprised to hear that her poor fatherless nephew is turning out so badly.

Marta is my aunt—my mom's half sister. She's at least sixty to my mom's thirty-eight, and she's lived in Australia for years. Mom says she went as far away as she could without sacrificing a country club membership. Aunt Marta comes back to Canada once in a while, but she hasn't visited us since we moved across the country from Lunenburg, Nova Scotia, to Victoria, British Columbia. We came here to be closer to my grandfather, who's ninety-five. He was a famous cellist, back in the day, and he never lets anyone forget it. Marta calls him "a monster of self-regard." Mom says he's just understandably self-involved, being so old and all. I don't know anyone else that old, so I don't know whether old age always goes hand in hand with rampaging egotism.

From what I can gather, he's always been that way, so my guess is that it's not an age thing. It's just Mom trying to put the best possible construction on a shitty situation, like she always does.

"I don't know what to do," she says now. "I need to find somewhere for him to go. Soon. Otherwise I'm going to have a breakdown. I mean it, Marta. Cart me away to the bin. Put me in a straitjacket. Give me a lobotomy. I don't care. At least I'd get some rest."

Somewhere for me to go? What's she talking about? I hate it here, but the only place I want to go is back to Lunenberg. I mean, I can't help it that I'm home all the time. I got mono right after Christmas, and by the time I was feeling better, school was about to close for spring break and then Easter. I'd missed so much school that I was able to convince Mom to let me finish the year by correspondence. And yeah, I'm alone a lot. Back home I had a few really good friends, guys I grew up with, but here—no one. Not yet anyway. Mom says it's early days, but she's wrong. I just don't have the energy for a social life. Or the interest. Even before I got mono, I couldn't muster up any desire to go to a movie, say, or a hockey game. Not that anyone asked. So the days slip by. A little schoolwork, a little TV, a little music, a lot of sleep. Some food, preferably microwavable. I don't have meals with my mom. Even when I was little, I hated eating with other people. I hate seeing all that half-chewed crud when they talk or laugh. Nobody has any manners. My mom used to laugh and call me Little Lord Fauntleroy. Now she sighs and turns away from me as I stomp downstairs with my dinner.

It's not like she's around much anyway. In spring and summer she's usually out the door by eight o'clock at the latest, working in other people's gardens until early afternoon. She comes home, has a shower and eats something before her piano students start arriving at about three. Some nights the Bach-bashing goes on until nine o'clock. Mom snacks in between students. She eats standing up, staring at her reflection in the window above the kitchen sink. If I stood beside her, this is what I would see: one tall, pale, bony person (me); one short, tanned, wiry person (her). Same stringy hair, same brown eyes, same wide mouth. Same great teeth, but you can't see mine because I'm not smiling. Different noses. Mine is a beak. Hers is small and veers slightly to the right when she smiles. Apparently I have the Jenkins nose, whatever that means. On weekends she works in our garden and practices the piano. And now she says she can't take it anymore and she wants to get rid of me. Harsh.

"I know we can't afford anything fancy," Mom is saying. "It just has to be clean." She's silent for a minute, her fingers playing a fugue on the placemat. She always does that when she's anxious. Plays Bach on a phantom piano. Maybe Aunt Marta is suggesting that I be shipped off to a detention center or something. Except I haven't done anything criminal. Yet. Mom says, "Uh-huh.

Uh-huh. Maybe you're right. No, I don't think he's drinking a lot. I do all the shopping and he never asks for wine or anything. Yes, I suppose he could call one of those Dial-a-Bottle places."

Drinking. Right. I'm sixteen. I have no friends. I have no money. The only alcohol in the house is a bottle of Kahlúa that my mom occasionally spikes her after-dinner coffee with. I drank some once and it almost made me puke. Give me a beer any day. How would I get drunk? Even if I wanted to, I just can't be bothered.

"I don't know about drugs. I don't think so." Mom sounds dubious. "I never see any of the signs." As if she would notice if I was stoned. I used to smoke up with my buddies back home—we'd come back to my place all chatty and hungry, and she was so happy that I had friends over that she'd make us brownie sundaes or blueberry pancakes. I have no idea how to score here, and it wouldn't be any fun alone anyway.

Mom is still talking. "The only other thing to do is hire someone to come to the house. Maybe not for the whole day—he sleeps so much—but at least to help out with meals."

What is she talking about? A babysitter? She must be totally losing it. Early-onset Alzheimer's or something. I'd choose a detention center over a babysitter any day. And I don't need help with meals. My microwaving skills are of a very high order.

"And someone has to help him take a shower."

I can't believe what I'm hearing. Since when do I need help taking a shower? I bound up the last four stairs and burst into the kitchen. I hit my head on the doorjamb on the way up and have to sit down suddenly until the wave of pain and dizziness passes. I have done this so many times since we've lived here that Mom doesn't even look up. You'd think I'd learn. When I can speak, my voice comes out as a croak. "No way, Mom. No fuckin' way."

"Hang on, Marta. Rolly's just come upstairs," she says calmly. She gives me a look that means *We'll talk later*. "Rolly, you know how I feel about swearing. I'm on the phone right now."

"Don't call me Rolly," I mutter, my teeth gritted. My head is exploding.

She covers the phone with her hand and hisses at me. "What's the matter with you?"

"I'm not going to some juvie prison, and there's no way I'm having a babysitter. If that's the way you're gonna play this, I'm outta here." I get up to go back downstairs, but my mom grabs my arm and hangs on.

"Juvie prison? Who said anything about juvie prison? What have you been up to? Are you in trouble?" She frowns and says into the phone, "Marta, I'll have to call you back."

For a small woman, my mom is really strong. She could probably bench-press me if she felt like it. I pull my arm away, rubbing the spot where she held me. There'll be bruises tomorrow.

"Rolly...Royce. I know it's been hard on you... moving here...starting at a new school...getting sick..."

"But, Mom—"

"Let me finish, Royce. I wish I could spend more time with you and I wish you'd make some friends, but there's only so much that I can do."

"I'll get a job. I'll help out more. Just no babysitter."

"Babysitter?"

"I heard you talking to Marta about sending me away. Or getting a babysitter."

Mom crosses her arms on the table and rests her head in her arms. Her hair falls around her face and her shoulders start to shake.

"Jeez, Mom. Don't cry," I say. "It's gonna be okay." It seems like the right thing to say, even though I have no idea if it's true. My head hurts too much to think straight.

No answer. Just a hiccup and a snort, followed by a sort of neigh. She's starting to freak me out, so I poke her shoulder and she lifts her face from her arms. There are tears on her cheeks and some snot under her nose, but she isn't crying; she's laughing the way she does when I do my fat Elvis impersonation for her.

"What's so funny?" I ask. I should be glad she's laughing, but I don't like being laughed at. Especially when I'm not trying to be funny.

"You," she replies, between gasps. "What did you think? That I was sick of you?"

"Uh, yeah."

"Oh, honey," she says. "Never." She snorts again. "Well, almost never."

"Then who were you and Marta talking about?"

She stops laughing and wipes her nose on the sleeve of her sweater. "Your grandfather."

I think about that for a minute. Since we've been here, Mom has visited her father every other day and called him every evening. On the weekends, she cooks all his dinners for the following week. She does his laundry and his grocery shopping. She cuts his hair. The few times I'd been to see him, he'd seemed fine to me. Old and cranky, but fine. Mind you, he never actually talks to me. He looks at me, grunts and goes back to whatever he's watching on TV. He bitches about Mom's cooking. Or the way she makes his bed. Or the kind of toothpaste she buys him. Now that I think about it, I can see why she might want to put him in a home.

When I went to visit him with Mom about a month ago, the first thing he said to me was, "You look like crap."

Coming from an ancient geezer in baggy brown cords, a stained beige sweater and slippers with the toes cut out, I though that was pretty rich.

"Right back atcha, Gramps," I said.

We glared at each other for a few seconds before he turned to my mother and said, "You need to get married again. The boy needs a man around the house. Someone to take him in hand. You're obviously not up to the job."

Mom and I walked past him and up the stairs to the kitchen, where we put away his groceries in silence. Mom's lips were pressed together in a straight, hard line as she slammed the cans of soup into the cupboard and flung the milk into the fridge. When we were finished, she turned to Arthur, who had followed us into the kitchen, and said, "See you next week."

"Can't you stay for a few minutes?" he whined. "Make me a coffee?"

She shook her head. "Errands to run. Sorry."

"What about you, boy?" he said. "Know how to make coffee?"

"Nope," I said. "No man around to teach me."

We left, with Arthur shouting after us that we were both useless, selfish parasites. I haven't been back.

"So what are you gonna do?" I ask now.

"I'm not sure yet," she says. "If we had a bigger place, maybe he could live with us." She shudders. My head is throbbing and I feel sick to my stomach. Maybe I have a concussion or maybe it's the thought of living with Grandpa.

"I'll just have to find a caregiver, I guess," Mom says. "He'll love that."

"Better find one with a high tolerance for verbal abuse," I say.

"You got that right," Mom replies.

As I turn to go downstairs, she adds, "And I hope you meant what you said about getting a job."

Two

Before I go any further, I should fill you in on a few things. First of all, my name is Royce Peterson. I have no middle name. When I was twelve, I started a campaign to add Isaac or Ichabod to my name so that my initials would be R.I.P., but Mom wouldn't sign off on it. She said two names were enough. When I was a baby, my dad started calling me Rolly (Rolls Royce, get it?) and it stuck. Now the whole family calls me that, and everyone but me still thinks it's cute. When we moved to Victoria, I made my mom promise to start calling me Royce. I didn't want a repeat performance of what happened in Lunenburg when I was six and the kids at school called me Roly-Poly, which didn't even make sense, since I was (and am) built like a stalk of bamboo. Skinny, with knobby bits.

Anyway, my mom's name is Nina and my dad's name was Michael. He died when I was two. Went for a run after dinner one summer evening and got slammed by a drunk driver. Died on the spot. I don't remember him at all. I used to think that I had some memories of him, but then I realized that all my supposed memories were just fantasies I had constructed from pictures in our photo album. Dad at the beach, throwing a Frisbee for a dog we used to have. Dad in the backyard, digging a flower bed for my mom. Dad tending a fire at a campsite by a lake. Dad after a run. I can smell the ocean, the damp soil, the smoke from the campfire, his sweat. I can feel his stubble on my cheek when he kisses me good night. But it's all crap, no matter how much I want it to be otherwise.

My mom was only twenty-four when my dad died. Her father was god-knows-where and her only sibling was in Australia. Marta's married to a banker named Horst, and they have six children and a bunch of grandchildren. They all play tennis. And golf. Some of the guys play polo, if you can believe it. Not water polo, which would be dumb enough. Real polo. The kind with horses. They have year-round tans and so far none of them has skin cancer. All my cousins but the youngest one—Mandy, who's about twenty—are a lot older than me. I met a couple of them—the twins, Chris and Rick—when they came to Canada for some extreme sports event when I was about ten. Mountain biking or snowboarding or hang gliding. I forget which. I've blocked it from my mind. They scared the crap out of me with their multi-pocketed hiking shorts, their mirrored shades, their wooly socks and their hairy calves. They called me "mate" and tried to talk my mom into sending me out to Australia so they could take me snorkeling on the Great Barrier Reef. Make a man out of me. Introduce me to barracudas and sharks. When Mom told them I couldn't swim, their bright blue eyes widened and their identical cleft chins dropped. "We're gobsmacked, bloody gobsmacked," they said in unison. The next day they took their muscles up to the top of some mountain, and I haven't seen them, or any of my other cousins, since. If they asked me now, I might go to Australia. I might even learn to swim when I got there. I'd have to draw the line at polo—horses terrify me—but at least I'd be away from here.

My mom never knew her mother. My dad's family lives in South Africa, so they weren't much help after Dad died. The occasional birthday present. A Christmas card or two. So Mom started earning money doing the two things she was good at: teaching piano and gardening. I was always with her—in a bassinet beside the piano, in a playpen in a client's garden. She saved on daycare and I got an overdose of classical music and sunshine.

I never met my mom's father until we moved here. Arthur was close to eighty when I was born. He told my mom that his traveling days were over, so he never came to visit us, even though he could afford it.

He never offered to fly us out to Victoria either. Never remembered birthdays or Christmas. I guess we weren't sufficiently interesting or useful to him. That all changed in late October when he had a small stroke and ended up in the hospital. Mom, who was listed as Arthur's next-of-kin, got a call from a doctor in Victoria who said Arthur was going to be sent home soon, but he couldn't drive anymore or cook his own meals or look after the house. For two weeks after his release from hospital, he would have twenty-four-hour care, paid for by his health insurance. After that, he was someone else's problem. Marta was too far away and too busy with her tennis and her banker and all her children and grandchildren. Mom only had me and a few piano students. And a shitload of guilt, it turns out.

We packed everything up, said goodbye to our friends and drove across the country in our old Audi wagon. It wasn't much of a road trip. Not like in the movies. Before we left Nova Scotia, I took a vow of silence that lasted until Saskatoon, where I broke down and begged for a burger rather than the sandwiches Mom made in our crappy motel room every night. She may have been enjoying the quiet for all I know, but all she said was, "McDonald's okay with you?" After that, it took more effort to stay silent than to talk, so the western provinces went by pretty quickly.

By the time we were on the ferry to Vancouver Island, I was positively giddy (for me). I stayed outside for the whole trip, watching for whales, taking pictures for Japanese tourists on their expensive digital cameras, covering my ears when the ship's whistle blew. Another ferry passed us, dangerously close it seemed to me, and I waved at a guy who was leaning over the railing of the other ship. He didn't wave back. I flipped him off, but then I realized that he was puking. Oops. A woman in a red jacket stood behind him, arms crossed, watching him vomit.

My mom had joined me on the deck, the wind whipping her ponytail into her face. She squinted at the couple on the other ferry and grinned. "Good times," she said. "At least you're not a puker."

"You know me," I said. "Stomach of steel."

A hair was stuck to her lipstick and she brushed it off. "I'm sorry about this, Rolly. The move. Your grandpa. I know it's hard for you. But I couldn't just leave him on his own. He raised me. Just because we're not close now doesn't mean he didn't do his best."

"Right," I said. "His best was live-in nannies, boarding schools and summer camps. What a guy."

"He had no choice," she protested. "My mother left us when I was three months old. He had to go where there was work. He couldn't very well take a baby on tour, could he? And he was in great demand. Berlin, New York, Paris. Everyone wanted the great Arthur Jenkins. There just wasn't enough Arthur to go around. So I did without."

"Bitter much?" I said.

She glared at me and turned to go inside. "Not as bitter as he is," she said.

Now, after a couple of months of catering to his every whim, she's interviewing caregivers and considering the seniors' equivalent of boarding school. No privacy, bad food and inmates who wet the bed. Tit for tat, Grandpa. What goes around, etc., etc.

Mom interviews about a dozen applicants before she finds one she likes even a little bit. A tiny woman who looks like she's about eighty herself, prides herself on getting her "old gents" squeaky clean "down there." Gross. One guy arrives on a huge chopper. He has a shaved head and a lot of prison tats—all blue, all nasty. He says he only looks after "old straight white dudes" and he always has to have Mondays off for his "meetings." Mom looks him in the eye and tells him that Grandpa is black (which he definitely isn't) and gay (ditto) and Jewish (I'm not sure, but with a name like Jenkins I doubt it). Biker dude stomps off, muttering about kikes, fags and niggers. "Nazi creep," Mom says.

By the time Mavis arrives, Mom is desperate. Mavis is a retired nurse, British, with a faint white mustache, stained teeth and muscular forearms. She says she has lots of experience with "old folks" and that she's sure Mr. Jenkins is a "poppet." Not bloody likely, I want to say.

She also claims to like "a bit of Brahms over tea," which endears her to Mom, and she is so much better qualified than any of the other applicants that Mom gives her the job on the spot. No reference check, which seems unwise to me.

She starts work the next day, and Grandpa, predictably, hates her on sight. Refuses to talk to her or eat her cooking. I could have told Mom that Grandpa, even though he's really old, would still want to be looked after by someone young and hot, but since no one of that description applied for the job, I didn't think she would find my opinion helpful. He phones Mom on her cell about twenty times that first day, raving about cutting her out of his will. Telling her how ungrateful she is. He even compares himself to King Lear, which I guess makes Mom Cordelia, the good daughter. Which probably makes me the Fool. He calls Mavis an old cow, a dyke and a sadist (apparently she cooked him something called Spotted Dick). Two days later Mavis quits, and Mom starts the whole process again.

This time she gets lucky right away. Lily is from the Philippines, she's trained as a care aide and she's super-motivated, since she's trying to save money to bring her husband and kids to Canada. She doesn't know anything about classical music, but she laughs a lot, she's tattoo-free (at least as far as I can see) and she's clearly not a dyke. She asks for Sundays off to go to church. That's it. She's happy to work six days a week, twelve hours a day, happy being the operative word. I've never met anyone who laughs so much with so little reason.

"She's perfect," Mom says after Lily leaves. "Dad will absolutely love her."

"Yeah, right," I say, imagining him grabbing Lily's ass as she brings him his lunch.

For a minute Mom looks as if she is in pain. Maybe she's reliving some past injury or it might simply be a leg cramp. Her father never remarried after her mother took off. She's not even sure her parents were ever married, but according to Mom, he always had a female companion when she was growing up. He'd turn up for lunch twice a year at her boarding school with Carmen or Graziella or Therese. All much younger than him, all musicians. He particularly liked singers. None of them came a second time. And now Mom has sent a sweet, youngish, relatively attractive woman into the dragon's den.

"I'm sure it'll be fine," she says. "Dad is far too old…"

I snort.

"And Lily's married, Royce."

"What does that have to do with anything?" I ask.

Two weeks later, Lily is history. Apparently Grandpa flashed her, and not just at bath time. The first few times, she laughed it off, but when he asked her to sit on his naked lap, she ran out of the house, called my mother and quit.

"I guess I'm lucky she hasn't filed charges." Mom is on the phone to Marta the day after Lily quits. I sit across the table from her in the kitchen, trying to guess what Marta is saying. Nothing good, from the look on Mom's face.

"I can't ask him to do that," she says. "And I can't afford to take the time off work. Not now. Not ever. And even if I could, I'd kill Dad within a week." She forces a laugh, but she's still frowning. Her hair looks like mine: dull, flat and stringy. The only difference is that she pulls hers back into a ponytail when she's working outside. Ponytails on guys are lame. She stands up and starts pacing the kitchen: sink, fridge, stove, table, sink, fridge, stove, table.

"I'll think about it, Marta," she says. "He won't like it."

Marta must say some Australian equivalent of *tough shit*, because Mom starts yelling, "Why don't you send Mandy, Marta? You said yourself she needs a change of scene—a challenge. Why do Royce and I have to deal with this? God knows, you've got the money. And the time. Why don't you hang up the tennis racquet for a season? Marta? Marta?" She holds the phone away from her face and stares at it as if it's a dead rat. "She hung up on me! Can you believe it? Sixty years old and she hung up on me?"

I shrug. I don't have any siblings, not even half ones. I have no idea why siblings fight. I'm about to head downstairs, when she says, "You know what Marta thinks?"

I shake my head. It can't be good. "What?"

"She thinks you should look after him."

Now it's my turn to be gobsmacked. I knew that word would come in handy one day. "Why me?" I squeak. "He hates me."

"Don't be ridiculous, Rolly. He doesn't hate you. He doesn't know you. You're not sick anymore, you're not in school, you're not doing anything, you don't have a job and I need the help. Maybe Marta's right. Maybe it would be good for you. I don't know."

"Good for me," I echo. "In what way?"

"Money, self-respect, something to put on your resume? Pick one. Would you prefer that we move in with him? Or have him move in here with us? Either way we'd be at his beck and call all day, every day. And you'll still have to get a part-time job. I hear McDonald's is always hiring. Or you can go over to his house for a few hours five days a week. Your choice. And it wouldn't be forever—just until school starts in the fall. By then I'll have had a chance to work something else out."

"How many hours a day?"

"Six, to start."

"How much money?"

"What I was paying the others—fifteen an hour."

"Cash?"

She sighs. "Yes. Cash."

"Who's paying?"

"He is." She doesn't elaborate. I've never thought about it before, but I guess he's loaded.

I do the math: $90 a day, 5 days a week. $450 a week, tax free. $1800 a month for 4 months. $7200. No way I'd make that flipping burgers or pumping gas. By the end of the summer, I'll have more than enough to buy a car and drive back to Nova Scotia. I'd fly, but I'm phobic. Bad experience in a small plane when I was ten.

"Until September then. Cash every Friday."

Mom nods.

"I'll take it under advisement," I say.

She nods again. "You do that," she says. "You've got an hour." She goes into the living room, sits at the piano and starts to play. Something slow and sad—Satie, I think, or Debussy. I always get those two mixed up. I know better than to interrupt her. She tells people she can't afford therapy, which is why she plays the piano and works in the garden. She sent me for therapy right after we got here, because she thought I might be depressed. I went a few times, just to get her off my case, and then I got mono and couldn't go anymore. She hasn't suggested it again. It's pretty expensive, and I'm not suicidal or anything. Just, as the therapist said, suffering from emotional dislocation. Otherwise known as homesickness. But now, as the liquid notes saturate the walls of the house, I envy her. What would it feel like to retreat into sound or scent, to feel soothed by a Chopin nocturne or calmed by a stand of hollyhocks?

The closest I get is when we have waffles and bacon with maple syrup.

Having my grandfather here would ruin everything. No question. When you're in the same room as him, it feels as if he is breathing all the air. He likes the curtains closed and the heat cranked up. He can't listen to music without criticizing the performers. He doesn't eat what he calls "foreign" food, even though he's spent so much time in exotic places. He must have been a treat to travel with. So I weigh it out in my mind. Him in my space all the time, or me in his six hours a day. Minimum wage, a dorky uniform and smiling at people I ordinarily wouldn't talk to versus one cranky old guy, one happy mom and cash. Quite a lot of cash. Enough to get me back home.

I wait until Mom stops playing before I go into the living room. She is sitting, shoulders hunched, looking at her hands on the keys. Her fingernails are crusted with dirt and there are small cuts on her wrists and the backs of her hands. Not the hands of a musician, Arthur said to her a while ago.

"Mom?" She looks up when I speak. "You got yourself a deal."

Three

Mom drops me off at Grandpa's house the next morning on her way to one of her gardening jobs. I haven't been up this early in months. Mom's in a good mood, so she lets me drive the truck, which is great until I stall at the Stop sign halfway up the hill to Grandpa's place. As I struggle with the gears and the clutch and the brake, we start to roll backward down the hill.

All she says is, "Relax, Rolly. Take your time."

I got my learners' license as soon as I turned sixteen, but Mom's usually too busy to take me out, and we can't afford driving lessons. I've never had to deal with a hill and a Stop sign before. It sucks.

I grind the gears and my teeth, and eventually we start going forward again. When we get to Grandpa's,

Mom reaches over and puts her hand on my arm as I set the brake.

"Do you want me to come in?" she asks.

I shake my head. "Nah. It's cool. He knows I'm coming, right?"

She nods.

"I'll figure it out. See you at two."

As I walk down the path to the front door, she calls out, "Bye, Rolly," before she drives off with a brief toot of the horn. I wave without turning around and walk up to the front door, clutching the key she's given me. I've never been here by myself. Should I ring the door-bell before I use the key? Or should I just walk in and risk giving him a heart attack? Before I can make up my mind, the door opens and there he is. Arthur Jenkins, celebrated cellist, legendary ladies' man, abysmal parent, shitty grandparent.

"Oh, it's you," he snarls. "Where's your mother?"

"Work," I reply. I try to slip by him into the house, but he's blocking the doorway with his walker. Something smells really bad—sour and burnt. "Uh, can I come in?"

"Why?"

Is the dementia this bad already? "I'm here to, uh, help you," I say.

"I don't need any help," he mutters. He turns around very slowly and walks away from me, leaving the door open. I stand on the doorstep, watching his progress, wondering if I should bail now and face my mom's wrath later. Fifteen an hour, I think, four hundred and fifty a week, eighteen hundred a month. It will be my mantra for the next four months. I step inside just as he says, "Can you make a decent cup of coffee?"

"Coffee? Yeah, I guess so. Unless you mean, like, a no-foam low-fat nutmeg cappuccino or something."

"I like a *café au lait* in the morning. Half coffee, half hot milk. Strong coffee. Think you can do that?"

"Yup."

"Not exactly loquacious, are you, boy?" he says. "Kind of taciturn. Although you probably don't know what I'm talking about." He snickers.

"No, I'm not loquacious. I prefer to think of myself as laconic," I say. "Taciturn seems a bit negative. And I think talking is overrated." Take the hint, old man, I want to say. Just shut up. It'll be better for both of us.

He snorts and shuffles into the living room where he maneuvers himself into a huge black leather office chair behind a glass-topped L-shaped desk. The desk and chair sit on an enormous red patterned rug. The effect is of Arthur sitting on an island with a population of one. It's the kind of desk that a CEO of some major corporation might have, and the whole arrangement faces a wall that features a gigantic wall-mounted plasma TV, tuned to CNN. In any other house, this might be an understandable arrangement, but if you opened the drapes, you would be looking at a hundred and eighty degrees of ocean, sky and mountains. There's even a small island with a lighthouse, and usually there's a sailboat or two, some fish boats, maybe a freighter going by. On clear days you can see right across to the Olympic Mountains. Mom says we'll go over there someday, soak in some hot springs she read about. The whole front of the house is floor-to-ceiling windows, but all the curtains are closed, and he sits with his back to the windows. The first time I was here, I opened the drapes and went out onto the wooden deck that runs from one end of the house to the other. Arthur freaked. I thought he was going to have a coronary. He's like a vampire—can't stand sunlight.

Next to the living room is the dining room, which is painted a sort of murky peach. The only furniture, if you can call it that, is a dusty grand piano with the lid down and the keys covered. Beyond that is the kitchen, which looks as if it hasn't been touched since the house was built. The breakfast nook comes complete with a yellow arborite table and matching chairs. Very retro. Down the hall from the living room is the master bedroom, which is paneled in dark wood. I've only been in there once when Mom sent me to gather up Arthur's dirty laundry. It was like being in a bear's winter den. Smelly, warm, claustrophobic. The outside of the house is white and curvy with a couple of porthole windows at the front. It's genuine Art Deco. Unique, very valuable and totally wasted on my grandfather, Mom says. Apparently he bought it sight unseen. His main requirement was privacy. The house is near the end of a dead-end street at the top of a hill. It sits on a huge rocky lot ringed with oak trees. You can't even see his neighbors' houses.

There's a brand-new Krups coffeemaker in the kitchen, and I discover the source of the sour smell: a saucepan of milk on the back burner has boiled over. It looks like it's been fermenting for a couple of days. I set the pan in the sink to soak and wash out the foil burner liner; then I dig around in the cupboards for a clean pan. There's milk in the fridge and coffee in a canister on the counter. There appears to be no dishwasher, which is very bad news. The mug that is sitting in the dishrack looks as if it has only ever been rinsed, never scrubbed. Good enough. When his coffee is ready, I take it to him in the living room. He takes a sip and sighs. Could be satisfaction, could be annoyance. It's impossible to tell.

"Mind if I open the drapes?" I ask. It's worth a try. I could look at that view all day.

"Yes."

"Yes, you mind, or yes, I can open them?"

"Yes, I mind."

"Oh."

"Too much glare on the screen."

"Oh," I say again. I can see his point. He turns up the volume on the TV and sips his coffee. I decide that I will open the curtains an inch or so every day and see if he notices.

After a few minutes, he looks at me and asks, "What are you still doing here?"

I shrug. "Beats me. Mom and Marta seem to think you need help. You look okay to me." I turn to go to the kitchen but stop when he lifts his coffee cup and says, "Another one of these, boy. And some ice cream."

"Ice cream? Now? It's, like, early."

"I'm ninety-five years old. I can have ice cream ten times a day if I want."

I shrug and say, "You're the boss." After I make him another *café au lait*, I scoop chocolate ice cream into a bowl, but when I get back to the living room, he is slumped sideways in his giant chair, snoring. I eat the ice cream and drink the coffee. It's a tasty combo, even at eight thirty in the morning.

While Arthur sleeps, I explore the rest of the house. There is another bedroom on the main floor, furnished with a single bed, an empty bookcase and a standing lamp. The curtains are dusty brown corduroy. Totally inviting. If you're a blind monk. Next to the bedroom is an ugly bathroom with stained pink fixtures and peeling floral wallpaper. Downstairs there is another drab bedroom, this one with an ancient television on a rickety table in front of an equally decrepit armchair. I turn on the TV, not really expecting it to work, but it comes on, tuned to the Weather Network. Everything's a bit green, but it's better than nothing. I sit down and feel around for a remote. No luck. All I find is a long thin wooden dowel with electrician's tape wrapped around one end. I realize the dowel just reaches from the chair to the TV. I poke at the channel change button on the TV, and now I'm watching someone decorate a cake that looks like a slot machine. Another jab and it's golf. Poking at the TV makes me laugh, so I do it again. And again. When my arm gets tired, I jab back to the Cartoon Network and settle down to watch *South Park*. I wonder if Arthur devised the primitive remote. If so, it's pretty cool. Very ingenious.

About ten minutes after I sit down, I hear bells ringing. I'm pretty sure it's not coming from the TV—although, being *South Park*, it could be—so I stick my head out the door. The sound is definitely coming from upstairs. I poke the TV off and head up to the living room, where I find that Grandpa has woken up in a less than fabulous mood. He is sitting in his chair, waving a brass bell shaped like a woman in a hoop skirt. When I appear, he roars, "Where's my ice cream?"

"Chill, Grandpa." I wrestle the bell away from him and put it on the piano. "You fell asleep. I'll get your ice cream."

"I wasn't asleep," he says. "You left me alone. I could have fallen."

"I was downstairs. Watching TV."

"Who said you could do that?" he says. When I don't reply, he announces, "I need to go to the bathroom. You shouldn't have let me drink so much coffee."

I shake my head. I'm beginning to see what Mom was talking about. He's a total jerk.

"Don't just stand there, boy. Help me up."

I position his walker next to the chair, swivel him around and grasp his forearms to try to pull him up. It's the first time I've been this close to him, and it's not a pleasant experience. He is skin and bones under his grubby old-man cardigan, and he smells pretty funky. I don't even want to think about the origin of the smell. There is dried drool on his chin and big flakes of dead skin rest on the collar of his plaid shirt. Tufts of hair are growing out of his ears. I pull slowly on his arms, and he staggers to his feet, swearing at me as he grabs the walker's handles.

"I'll have bruises tomorrow," he mutters as he begins the trek to the bathroom. "Even that cow Mavis knew how to get me out of my chair."

I put my hand out to steady him as he passes, and he swats at me with one arthritic claw. When he loses his balance and starts to fall, I grab him under the arms and set him upright again, surprised at how heavy he feels. Deadweight, that's what it's called.

"Get your hands off me," he grunts.

"No problem," I reply.

It's going to be a very long summer.

Somehow I make it through the next five hours. Watching the old TV downstairs, napping in the monk's cell. Every time I find a show I want to watch or I nod off, he rings the bell and yells for me. He wants a drink, he wants food, he wants his nail clippers, he wants a list that he swears is posted on the refrigerator, he wants a particular pen. Everything I do is wrong. The drink is too cold or too hot or too sweet or not sweet enough. The grilled cheese sandwich I make him for lunch is too brown and has too much cheese. The soup is lumpy. The nail clippers are dull. The list is nowhere to be found and the pen has run dry. Except for trips to the bathroom, he sits in his chair, staring at the TV. He flips back and forth between CNN and MTV. He hates all news anchors, especially the female ones, but he's a big fan of the Pussycat Dolls.

When he says, "I'd like a piece of that," I'm pretty sure he's not talking about Nancy Grace. He leans forward in his chair to get a closer look at a blond woman in thigh-high stiletto boots, fishnet stockings held up by a black lace garter belt, sequined short-shorts and a silver bustier. She's totally hot, in a skanky sort of way. I agree with Arthur—I, too, would like a piece of that, but I'm not about to share that with him.

"They look like hookers," he chortles. "Cheap hookers. No class. But you wouldn't know about that, would you, boy? Still a virgin, I bet."

Wouldn't you like to know, old man, I think. No way I'm telling him that the furthest I got was a blow job from Georgia ("Peaches") Millman last year at my going-away party. Peaches and I grew up together. We lived on the same street and went to the same school. Her best friend was dating my best friend. She was like her nickname: round and juicy and sweet. We hung out all the time, usually with other people, but sometimes we'd cut class and come back to my house and watch movies and make out. I wish I'd had a chance to make our relationship official, although I'm not really sure how you do that—cheap jewelry, red roses, a candlelit dinner and a romantic movie? None of that felt right, so I did nothing other than try to get her to take off her bra. Maybe the blow job was Peaches' way of sealing the deal. Even if it wasn't, it was pretty effective. She was one of the main reasons I wanted to get back to Lunenburg, even if I had to hitchhike. There was nothing for me here. Unless you counted a cranky, shriveled-up old man.

Arthur swivels his chair to look at me and, maybe it's my imagination, but I think he winks at me before he turns back to the TV. Winking freaks me out. Always has. Mom says that when I was little I had night terrors about someone I called The Winking Man. Come to think of it, he kinda looked like Arthur. I shudder and try to think about something else. I wonder whether Arthur was still a virgin when he was my age. In 1931. Hard to imagine. According to Mom, he was a musical prodigy with a mane of dark red hair, which he wore in a style she calls leonine. In other words, long and swept back from his face, like Charlton Heston as Moses or Kenny Rogers circa 1980. His eyes are a very pale acid-wash blue, with a dark ring around the iris. His hair is still long but it's faded to the color of melted orange sherbet, and it's so greasy I can see comb marks in it. I run my hands through my own hair and vow to wash it as soon as I get home.

By the end of my workday, the sink is full of dirty dishes, and I can smell the garbage under the sink. I risk pulling the kitchen curtains back and cracking open a window, but he feels the draft, even two rooms away.

"Shut that window, boy," he yells. "You trying to kill me?"

Fortunately he can't see me nod. I follow the instructions Mom has given me: I put his frozen dinner in the microwave so he can nuke it later. I'm supposed to set the table, but I figure he can wash a knife and fork. At two o'clock, Mom phones to say she's on her way.

"Gotta go, Grandpa," I say. "See you tomorrow."

He grunts. "Don't call me Grandpa, boy. Makes me feel old."

I stare at him. He's ancient. Wrinkled, stooped, gnarled. Forgetful, rude, smelly. How could he feel anything but old?

"Well, don't call me boy, then," I say. "I'm not your slave. And don't call me Rolly either. My name's Royce."

We glare at each other for a moment. I can think of a lot of things to call him, none of them complimentary. I hear Mom honk, and as I turn to leave, he says, "Call me Arthur."

"Okay," I say. "Arthur it is."

He grunts again, and I'm outta there.

Four

I spend the first week of my servitude watching reruns, burning sandwiches, eating ice cream and snooping. When I find a full bottle of Scotch in the back of one of the kitchen cupboards, I take it home with me. Arthur is enough to drive anyone to drink. I wish it was beer, but, as Mom always says, beggars can't be choosers. I also find cans of soup with expiration dates from before I was born, and bottles of soy sauce from the Ming dynasty. One morning, when I'm rooting around in the extra bedroom upstairs, I discover a state-of-the-art (for 1970) Bang & Olufsen stereo system under the bed. In the cupboard, under some old blankets, are boxes and boxes of CDs, cassettes and LPs, many with Arthur's photograph on the cover. A lot of them are still factory sealed. Even though I know he was famous, this is the first time

I realize just how famous he was. He recorded with people even I've heard of: Yehudi Menuhin, Pablo Casals, Yo-Yo Ma. And now he listens to rap and hip-hop and the Pussycat Dolls, for fuck's sake. You'd think it would be torture for someone like him. When I think about it, I realize that there is nothing in the house, besides the piano, that would give away the fact that a musician lives here. No photographs, no instruments, no mementos from his travels. He might as well have been an accountant. Or a hit man. That's more Arthur's style.

Before I have a chance to put the stuff back in the cupboard, the bell rings and he yells for me. I go into the living room, where he has muted the TV and sits glowering at his twisted hands, as if they are responsible for his current sorry-ass state.

"I need a shower," he announces.

I've been dreading this moment. I have no idea what to do, or how much help he requires—Mom's instructions were vague. "Just follow his lead," she said. Like we're doing the tango. I get him out of his chair, and we totter down the hall toward his bedroom, which has an adjoining bathroom with a walk-in shower.

When I try to come into the bathroom with him, he brushes me away as if I were a mosquito.

"This is as far as you go, boy. Just stand outside the door in case I fall. And bring me some fresh towels. No one ever changes the towels. It's like drying yourself with a sheet of plywood."

I find some clean towels in a hall cupboard and pass them in to him. In a few minutes the shower starts, and I stand outside the door, praying that he doesn't slip on a bar of soap. Mom will be pissed if he gets hurt. After a while, I get bored and start looking around the room, which is illuminated by a single bug-encrusted ceiling fixture. There are dirty clothes everywhere. Mom hasn't said anything about doing laundry, so I don't touch them. There are bottles of pills on the bedside table—Valium, Dulcolax, Tylenol, low-dose Aspirin, Synthroid, a multivitamin—and numerous glasses of scummy water. I'm considering boosting the Valium when Arthur comes out of the bathroom in a gray flannel bathrobe. His hair is dripping onto the collar of the robe, which isn't tied shut. I get a quick flash of scrawny white thighs and a caved-in chest before he turns away from me and struggles with the belt. Maybe this is how it all started with Lily, although I doubt he'll be asking me to sit on his lap.

"Clean clothes," he barks. "Get me some clean clothes."

I find socks and underwear in a dresser drawer; shirts and pants are hanging up in the closet. He shoos me away as he sits on the bed and pulls up his briefs. While he dresses, which takes a really long time, I try to figure out how much money there is in a jar of change on his dresser. He has trouble with his socks, but there's no way I'm going to risk slitting my wrists on his gnarled toenails, and I'm not about to suggest a session with the clippers. After a few minutes of struggle, he tosses the socks on the floor and jams his bare feet into his toeless slippers. Then he towels his hair a bit and runs a filthy black rat-tail comb through it.

"Ever wash that comb, Arthur?" I ask.

"None of your business, boy," he replies as we make our way back to the living room.

"We had a deal, Arthur. Remember? About my name?"

"I'm old, but I'm not an idiot, Royce," he says. "I remember. Now get me some ice cream."

By the end of the first week, I've explored most of Arthur's house. My most significant discovery is a brand-new MacBook Air, which I find in his desk drawer one afternoon when he's in the bathroom. There's only one file on the hard drive: a document entitled *Me*. The document is blank. Hard to believe Arthur has nothing to say on that topic.

When Mom picks me up on Friday, she comes in to say hello to Arthur, who is ensconced in his usual place, watching Anderson Cooper on CNN.

"Faggot," he yells at the screen. "I knew your mother. Gloria Vanderbilt. Skin and bones. Married that bastard Stokowski."

"Hey, Dad," Mom says. "Royce looking after you okay?"

Arthur turns away from the screen and grimaces at me. If I didn't know better, I might almost think it was a smile. Mom calls Arthur's smile an endangered species—as dangerous and elusive and powerful as a snow leopard or an angel shark and so rarely seen as to be mythical.

"That's good then," Mom says, as if he has spoken.

"See you Monday, Arthur," I say as I pick up my pack in the kitchen. "Your dinner's in the microwave." I start toward the door, anxious to get away from him and get my money from Mom, but his voice stops me before I reach the door.

"You don't care, either of you. I'm just a nuisance, an old, used-up, useless piece of garbage. I'd be better off dead." His voice has a quality I haven't heard before—self-pitying, needy.

"Oh, Dad," Mom sighs. She's still in the living room, and now she's crouching beside his chair, stroking his arm. "You know that's not true. I'll be here tomorrow. Maybe we can go for a drive. Get a coffee and sit by the ocean."

He shakes his head sorrowfully, as if to say, "What's the point?" and I want to scream at Mom, "He's playing you. He's fine. It's a guilt trip." She's always telling me how manipulative he is, how he always gets his own way, but she still buys into it. Like the time he told her he was having chest pains so she wouldn't go away for the weekend with her friend Carol. Turns out he needed his house cleaned because some old girlfriend from Budapest was coming to stay. Mom swore she wouldn't fall for his bullshit again, but I guess old habits die hard.

"We'll talk about it tomorrow," Mom says. "I'll be here bright and early. Okay?"

She straightens up and leans over to kiss him on the cheek. He pulls away, and she ends up kissing the air and patting his shoulder.

"Bye, Dad," she says.

"Later, dude," I call from the door.

Arthur picks up the remote, switches to MTV and cranks the volume. A woman's plaintive voice follows us out the door. *"You cut me open and I keep bleeding..."* I wonder if that's the way Mom feels.

When we get to the truck, Mom tosses me the keys. I hop into the driver's seat. As I do up my seatbelt, I look over at her and see that she is crying. Again.

Way to go, Arthur.

I start to tell her that Arthur's an asshole, but she waves my words away.

"Just drive," she mumbles. "I'll be okay."

We drive home in silence.

Saturday morning arrives and I wake up early, which is a piss-off, since I don't have to get up. I try to go back to sleep, but I can hear the shower running upstairs, and a few minutes later the fridge door opens and closes. Mom is up and on the move. I'm now awake enough to be hungry, so I head upstairs. Mom's at the kitchen table, sipping coffee and reading the Saturday *Globe*. She looks up as I come into the kitchen.

"It's Saturday, you know," she says. "You're not on duty."

I nod and pour myself a coffee, just to be sociable. With enough cream and sugar it's almost drinkable. I actually prefer the taste of tea, but it's not exactly the beverage of choice for sixteen-year-old guys. I stand leaning against the sink, wondering if there are any waffles in the freezer.

"Couldn't sleep," I tell her. "Thought I'd check out some cars today."

"Cars?"

"Yeah, you know? Four wheels, seats, internal combustion engine."

"You're going to look at cars? Why?"

She seems a little slow on the uptake today, for some reason. Maybe she needs more coffee. I pour a little more into her mug.

"I figure that if I work for four months, I'll have enough money to buy a pretty sweet car before I go back to school." I don't mention that the school I'll be driving to is in Nova Scotia. She's got enough on her plate already.

"A car, Rolly…" I glare at her and she says, "Royce. How will you insure it? Pay for gas? Cars are expensive to run, and I don't want you driving some heap of junk.

I'm not sure this is a good idea at all. How about just—
I don't know—saving the money?"

"Right, Mom," I say. "And I'm also going to cut my
hair and buy a pinstripe suit for the Young Investors'
Club annual retreat. Oh, and after that, I'm going to a
Tony Robbins motivational workshop."

"Okay, okay, I get it." She sighs. "Maybe save a bit of
it—ten percent? Make your old mother happy?"

"Ten percent, huh?" I do a quick calculation. Ten
percent ought to cover my insurance costs for a year.
"Maybe. Don't worry so much. I'm not gonna buy the
first beater I see. Research, research, research. You know
me. Remember how long it took me to choose a bike?"
My bike search was legendary—almost a year's worth of
Consumer Reports, online searches and test rides—but
I hardly ride it anymore since we moved here. Too many
hills. Not enough energy.

She gets up and puts her dishes in the sink. "I gotta
run," she says with a sigh. "The old coot awaits. Maybe
we can get pizza for dinner."

I feel bad that she has to spend her weekend with
Arthur, but not so bad that I offer to take her place.
I can't face another day with him. Monday morning will
roll around soon enough, I figure.

"Take a book, Mom," I say. "There's not much to do,
unless you like CNN and MTV."

"I'm going to take him out. He needs to do something other than stare at a television screen. I don't know

how long it's been since he left the house for anything other than a doctor's appointment."

"Good luck with that," I say, imagining the scene: Mom wrestling Arthur in and out of the truck; Arthur berating Mom about her driving, the price of a cup of coffee, the draft from her open window, her choice of career, her parenting skills.

After she leaves, I go back to bed and try to sleep, but the stupid song I heard at Arthur's is stuck in my head: *You cut me open and I keep bleeding...* I give up trying to rest and start a load of laundry. I've got no clean clothes. Mom announced last week that since I was feeling better, I could start doing my own laundry. I've been waiting her out, seeing if she would crack, but she hasn't. The pile of dirty laundry is now about the size of a Smart car. Four loads later, I'm tired, but I can't sit still, so I drag my bike out of the garage, pump up the tires and ride it down to the beach. It feels good to be back on the bike again. I'd forgotten I had thigh muscles and that the wind feels good on my face. I ride for half an hour and then nap for three hours. When Mom comes home I'm asleep on the couch in the living room beside a pile of folded laundry. When I wake up, she smiles at me and says, "What have you done with my son?"

Five

On Monday I ride my bike to Arthur's. Having mono has messed with my stamina though; a couple of times I have to get off the bike and push it up a hill. When I get there, he isn't in his usual spot in front of the TV. The surface of his desk is littered with crumpled and stained paper napkins, used Kleenex, an electric shaver, two flashlights, a collection of dried-up pens, a bird's skull, a plate of congealed scrambled eggs, three dirty coffee mugs, a keychain with about a dozen keys attached, two phones (one of them a brand-new cell), his address book and his checkbook. Nothing unusual there.

His walker is in the dining room, by the piano. I search the whole main floor: no Arthur. I even go out on the deck, half expecting to see—what? That he'd climbed the railing and hurled himself onto the rocks? Not really Arthur's style. No audience. I go downstairs, yelling as I run from room to room. No response. What the hell? If Arthur has croaked, there goes my summer job and my car. He better not be dead. Not yet anyway. Just as I am pulling out my cellphone to call Mom, I hear a car start, very close by. A door that has always been locked is slightly ajar, so I follow the sound into what turns out to be the garage. In the garage is a mint-condition 1956 black T-bird. In the T-bird is Arthur.

"Holy shit!" I yell over the sound of the engine. "Dude, what are you doing?"

Arthur looks up and beckons me over. He rolls down the window and says, "Can't let the battery die, *dude*. I start her up once a week. Don't tell your mother. She took away my license, you know."

I nod. Mom had literally wrestled the license out of his hands at the site of an accident where his car had jumped the curb and very nearly hit a little girl playing hopscotch on the sidewalk outside her house. The police who came to the scene found him parked on someone's lawn under a red maple. He was slurring his words, and at first they thought he was drunk. A breathalyzer test proved otherwise. His doctor said he might have had a small stroke or simply fallen asleep at the wheel. Either way, Arthur's driving days were over. I guess I had just assumed that the car had been sold. I'd never even seen it before today.

"That kid shouldn't have been out playing by herself," he says. "Parents made a huge fuss. Not a scratch on her."

"Close call though," I say. I remember how upset Mom was, how she sent flowers to the girl's family, even though the kid was more frightened than anything else. Mom apologized to them over and over, promising that her father would never drive again.

"I don't let just anybody touch this car," Arthur says. "A fellow from Vancouver comes over and takes care of her for me. Costs a fortune, but it's worth it. Tip-top shape, even now. Over fifty years old. Bought her off the lot, you know."

It takes me a minute to register that he means that the car wasn't damaged in the near-accident. He doesn't give a shit about the little girl.

As if he's reading my mind, he adds, "I gave them money, you know."

"What?"

"That kid's parents. Paid them off so they wouldn't go after me. Hope they used the money to hire someone to look after their kid—they sure weren't doing the job."

Coming from a man who virtually abandoned his own children, this seems pretty rich.

"She's still insured, you know," he continues, caressing the steering wheel. "I had my lawyer take care of that."

"But you can't drive, Arthur," I say. "No license—remember?"

He gazes up at me, and the expression on his face can only be described as crafty. Or demented. Or both.

"Maybe I can't drive," he says, "but you can."

I step back and hold up my hands as if he is training a gun on me.

"Whoa, Arthur. Back it up a bit. You want me to drive your car?"

"What's the matter, boy? Too much car for you? Not man enough?" I swear he cackles as he revs the engine.

"It's not that," I say. "It's…" I don't finish my sentence, because suddenly I can't think of a single reason why I shouldn't drive this amazing car. "I only have my learners' license. I mean, I have to drive with a licensed driver and you're not…"

"I doubt whether Nina cancelled it. It's probably sitting in a drawer somewhere. You could probably find it, if you looked around."

"So now you want me to snoop through my mom's stuff?"

"Not snoop, you pussy. Just find what's legally mine." He turns off the engine and drags his legs slowly out of the car. "Help me upstairs," he says. "And make me a cup of coffee."

Getting him back upstairs is a challenge. I don't even want to think about how he got down by himself. I'll say one thing for him—he's one determined old guy. He has to use the handrails on the stairs to pull himself up. I walk behind him, like a spotter for a very feeble gymnast in the geriatric Olympics. He farts a couple of times as we ascend, which makes us both laugh.

By the time I get him into his chair, a thin film of sweat covers his face, his hands are shaking and his breath is coming in short, shallow gasps. He orders me to make him a *café au lait*, but by the time I bring it to him, he is asleep, his head lolling at an uncomfortable angle. As I prop a pillow under his neck, I notice that he misses a lot of spots when he shaves and that the crevasses (they're too big to be called wrinkles) that bracket his mouth look sore. Nothing much I can do about that, so I drink his coffee and go off in search of amusement. I'm pretty bored, and lunch isn't for a few hours. If he really does want me to drive the car, I figure I'd better check it out.

I leave the door open when I go back into the garage. I'm not worried about Arthur finding me down here; he's way too tired to navigate the stairs again. I just want to be able to hear the bell if he rings it. The garage is warm and clean. It doesn't smell like moldy sports equipment or old paint or fertilizer like our garage back home in Nova Scotia. The floor isn't oil-stained and littered with dried-up leaves and grass clippings and dirt. There aren't any empty beer bottles or stacks of old newspapers or banged-up patio furniture. There isn't even a lawnmower, which makes sense because there isn't a lawn. There is just the car, a scarred wooden workbench with some open shelving above it and a single rake.

I walk around the car, admiring its Jetson-like lines, the round windows in its removable hardtop, the white-wall tires, the word *Thunderbird* in script on the fin. 1956. Arthur would have been—what? Early-forties? I imagine him in a tuxedo and a long white silk scarf, fresh off a European tour, his hair still red, holding open the passenger door for a woman who looks like Audrey Hepburn. For all I know, he fucked Audrey Hepburn. It's entirely possible. I open the driver's-side door and slide into the seat. The interior of the car smells showroom-fresh, as if it's never been off the lot. Maybe Arthur sprays it every week with some nasty ozone-destroying new-car-smell-in-a-can. I adjust the seat so my knees aren't hitting the steering wheel; then I put my hand on the gearshift knob and my foot on the clutch. Which is when I notice two things: it's a three speed transmission, not a five like I'm used to, and the keys are in the ignition.

Theoretically, I could open the garage door and drive away. Maybe it would be worth it, even if I got busted for driving without another licensed driver in the car. Then again, if I got busted, Mom would find out and she'd be pissed beyond belief. She'd fire me and make me get a job at McDonald's. No way I'd make enough to buy my own wheels. No way I'd get back to Lunenburg. So I sit in the T-bird, fondling the gearshift and pumping the clutch. Pretty soon I've drifted into a dream about pulling up in front of my old school in the T-bird. The first bell is ringing and someone is calling my name. "Royce! Royce! Goddammit, boy. Get up here." Oh, crap.

I take the scenic route home on my bike, enjoying the fact that I'm out on the road while everyone else is still in school. I arrive home sweaty and sore, take a shower and sit down in front of the TV with a Diet Coke and a bowl of nachos. It's not like I need diet drinks, but Mom thinks she does, so that's all she buys. I wonder what Arthur is watching, so I check out MTV and CNN. Lady Gaga or Larry King. Ugh. What Arthur really needs is that asshole Dr. Phil. Maybe he'd do an intervention, although it wouldn't be worth his time. Arthur isn't going to change.

After a few minutes of staring out the window, I get up and go to Mom's room. Her bed isn't made (bad Mom) and there are dirty clothes in a pile by the door. There's a stack of books on her dusty night table, along with her reading glasses and a glass of water (not scummy, I'm happy to report). I stand in the doorway, wondering where she would put Arthur's license. I pray it's not in with her underwear. I'm not going there. The most obvious place is the tiny desk that sits under the window. She has an old laptop and a printer that she uses for scheduling and billing her garden clients and piano students. Bills are in a wicker basket. There's a mug full of pens and a moldy cup of coffee on a coaster made from an old tile. The desk has two drawers. The top one is full of office supplies, the bottom one is obviously the "junk" drawer, although we have one in the kitchen too. Old rubber bands, push pins, recipe cards, take-out menus, string, a broken ruler, scissors, a pill bottle full of teeth (mine, I assume), an assortment of screws and picture-hangers, some gum, packages of photos and, lo and behold, at the very bottom, Arthur's license. Good picture. Even four years ago he didn't look as wrecked as he does now. I pocket the license, close the drawer and sneak out of Mom's room, feeling a weird combination of triumph and shame. No adrenaline rush, so I probably don't have a future as a criminal. Maybe I can point that out to Mom if she ever finds out I took the license.

The next day when I get to Arthur's, I make a big production of giving him the license, as if I had scaled Mt. Everest to get it. He simply grunts and says, "Where's my coffee?"

"You're welcome," I say. I mess around in the hall closet while he has his coffee. There are about fifteen jackets and coats on wire hangers: a red plaid lumber-jack shirt, a maroon velour leisure jacket, a classic beige trench coat, a brown corduroy jacket with leather elbow patches, tweed (lots of tweed), and an ancient, smelly Cowichan Indian sweater with a moose on the back. I slip on an awesome green leather bomber jacket circa 1972; the sleeves are too short, but the rest of it fits. I leave it on while I rummage around in a huge pile of hats on the shelf above the coats: four French berets, a grubby Tilley hat, three floppy-brimmed pastel cotton bucket hats, a tuque that matches the Indian sweater, a khaki cap with a flap to keep the sun off your neck, a suede fedora (which I put on), a tweed newsboy cap and a big straw Panama Stetson.

Behind the hats are about twenty photo albums. Each one has a date range written on masking tape stuck to the cover. I pull one out: 1955–1958. The black paper is flaking and the glue behind the pictures has dried up. A picture flutters to the floor just as Arthur summons me with the bell. Before I put the picture back in the album, I examine the woman standing beside Arthur in the photo. Is she my grandmother? Impossible to know. She is tall and curvy, with dark hair in an elaborate beehive, dark lipstick and large, even teeth. I turn the photo over and see a name: Coralee. Not my grandmother then. All I know about her is her name—Bella—and that she played the violin. My mother has no pictures, no keepsakes. Nothing.

When I get upstairs, Arthur takes in my jacket and hat. He snorts. "You look like a pimp."

"Thanks," I reply, "although I was sort of aiming for low-life, small-time drug dealer."

"That too," Arthur says. "Let's go for a ride."

"Now?"

"Yes—now. I'm bored. Get me a coat. One of the tweed ones. And a beret. And bring a box of Kleenex."

"Kleenex?" I shudder, envisioning unscheduled bathroom breaks at the side of the road.

"Drafts make me sneeze."

"Right," I say. "One tweed coat, one beret, one box of Kleenex, coming up."

Before we go, Arthur has to pee, brush his teeth and get down the stairs, this time with me in front of him. While he's in the bathroom, I tape a homemade *L* (for *Learner)* sign in the back window of the car. No sense tempting fate. Even though he seems stronger today, it still takes half an hour to get him down to the car and buckled into his seat.

He reaches into the glove compartment and pulls out the garage door remote.

"Where to?" I ask as the door rises behind us.

"Top Down."

"I thought you hated drafts. It's not very warm out yet." Not that I don't want to drive with the top down. It's just that I'd rather do it without him in the passenger seat.

Arthur slaps the dashboard with a gnarled, liver-spotted hand. "It's the name of a barbershop, boy. You need a haircut."

Six

nstead of arguing with Arthur, I concentrate on backing the T-bird out of the garage. That's when I discover that the car does not have power steering or power brakes or synchromesh. Or at least it feels as if there is no synchromesh when I shift. Just getting into reverse is a challenge. It doesn't help that every time I stall or grind a gear, Arthur swears and tries to wrestle the gearshift away from me. By the time I get the car out of the garage and into the driveway, I am sweating and my heart is racing. I take a moment to try to relax before I back out into the street.

"What are we waiting for, boy?" Arthur asks, turning in his seat and glaring at me.

"Waiting for you to stop being a jerk," I mutter.

"What?"

"Just making sure the gearshift works, Art. Don't want to wreck your car."

"Easy as pie," he says. "What's your problem?"

"No problem," I say as I miraculously manage to get us out onto the street and heading down the hill without grinding, stalling, crashing, or smacking Arthur.

"Take the ocean route," Arthur says when we get to the bottom of the hill.

I turn right, and we drive in silence along the waterfront. I'm starting to get the hang of the gears, and the car feels awesome. People gawk at us as we drive by, and Arthur waves at them, especially the young women.

"Car like this, boy, you get laid all the time," he says as we roll up to a Stop sign beside a really hot girl in a pink tank top and plaid short-shorts. She is walking a golden retriever and she gives the car a huge smile and a little finger-waggle. I wish I believed that she's smiling at me, but I know it's the car. Then Arthur cranks down his window (I'm surprised he has the strength) and says, "Ditch the dog and come for a ride with us, sweetheart." Her smile vanishes and she yanks on the dog's leash and jogs away, calling "Pervert!" over her shoulder.

"Good one, Arthur," I say.

"Pussy," Arthur replies.

I've never been to a barbershop—my mom cut my hair until I decided to let it grow—but I'm kind of expecting old guys, cigars, spittoons, scuffed lino on the floors and baseball on the radio. Top Down actually has one of those red-and-white-striped barber poles outside, but that's the only traditional thing about it. Inside there's track lighting, dark wood floors, black leather client chairs, a wall-mounted flat-screen TV, jazz coming out of hidden speakers, shelves of "product" and a proprietor who is tall, black and definitely female.

"Say hello to Kim, boy," Arthur says as she kisses him on both cheeks and does what can only be described as croon over him. He must tip well.

I stick out my hand to shake hers. "Contrary to what Arthur would have you believe, I do have a name. I'm Royce Peterson. His grandson."

"Pleased to meet you, Royce," she says. "Good-looking boy," she says to Arthur.

"Good genes," Arthur says.

"Now, what can I do for you boys?" Kim asks.

"He needs a haircut," Arthur says.

"So do you," Kim replies. She turns to me and strokes my hair. Her nails are long and red and her hand smells flowery, but with a whiff of something tangy—ammonia maybe, or peroxide. "Time for a change?" she asks me.

I shrug. "Maybe. What do you think?"

"Definitely," Kim says, leading me over to a shampooing station and draping a zebra-print cape over my shoulders. I lean back and close my eyes as she wets my hair and massages shampoo into my scalp. Her breasts are only inches from my face. It doesn't take long before I am deeply grateful for the voluminous cape covering my lap. When she is finished, we make our way over to a cutting station where I adjust myself surreptitiously while Kim assembles her tools and combs my hair. Arthur has taken up residence on a white leather couch and appears to be asleep.

"So...what were you thinking?" Kim asks.

"I wasn't. Arthur was."

"Arthur." She laughs. "What a character."

I nod at myself in the mirror as she runs her fingers through my wet hair. Her lips are pursed and she is frowning slightly, as if my hair is confusing her somehow.

"Take it all off," I say. I have no idea why I've grown my hair this long, and I have no idea how I know it's time to cut it off. I just do.

"You sure?"

"Yup. All of it. I want to see what my skull looks like."

"Just what I was thinking," Kim replies. "You have a beautiful skull. Let's get it out of hiding."

It doesn't take long. And as it turns out, I do have quite a shapely skull. She has left a bit of fuzz—for girls to touch, she says, although I have my doubts about that. I run my hands over the fuzz and stare at myself in the mirror. I look completely different—older, for sure, and tougher.

Arthur wakes up with a snort and glares at me.

"You joining the army, boy?"

"Oh, Arthur," Kim says. "Stop your nonsense. He's gorgeous. Just look at that shape." She glides her hand over my fuzzy head and gives a small shiver. "Gorgeous," she repeats. "Your turn now," she says as she helps Arthur to the shampoo station.

"Why don't you get yourself a coffee next door, Royce?" Kim says as she snugs the cape around Arthur's scrawny neck. "Just tell them to put it on my tab."

I nod and go to the coffee shop, where I'm pretty sure the barista, a guy about my age, is flirting with me while he makes my drink. It's not my scene, but even so I take it as confirmation that I've done the right thing. It's weird to feel the air on my scalp. Exposed, but also free. Free of what, I'm not exactly sure.

When I get back to the shop, Arthur is bald. Totally bald. No fuzz even. Shaved to the skin. Shiny. And grinning from ear to ear, which is almost as scary as his bald head. His teeth aren't exactly white. The term *death's-head* comes to mind.

"Holy shit, Arthur," I say.

"Holy shit, indeed, Royce," he says. "Where's my coffee?"

"Coffee?" Was I supposed to get him a coffee? I can't stop looking at his head. And mine. Side by side in the mirror I see something even scarier than his bald head: a family resemblance. My head is the same shape as his, from my wide, high forehead right down to a couple of prominent bumps at the base of my skull. Our noses are identical—the Jenkins beak. I run my hand over the back of my head and he cackles.

"Bonking bumps," he says.

"What?"

"They're called bonking bumps—the ones at the base of your skull. Size does matter. I had a girlfriend who believed in phrenology. We tested her theory—often."

Kim rolls her eyes and helps him out of the chair. He pats her ass, and she winks at me and says, "Runs in the family, then, does it?"

Who knew an entire head could blush? Or that a wink could be so welcome?

When we get home I give Arthur his lunch, and he sleeps for nearly two hours. When he wakes up, he is beyond grouchy. His head is cold and he insists on wearing the Cowichan tuque. He's also convinced that I shaved his head (and my own) while he slept. He has no recollection of going to Kim's shop or of telling her to turn him into a cue ball. He doesn't believe me when I tell him he let me drive the car.

I give up trying to persuade him otherwise and focus on calming him down with ice cream and bad television. He's branched out lately to watching reruns of *Little House on the Prairie* on some oldies cable channel. I'm in the kitchen putting his dinner together when he announces, "My father shaved our heads every summer."

"How come?" I ask.

"Prairie summers were hot. Blazing hot. We spent most days in the swimming hole. Naked and bald, swinging from ropes. Girls weren't allowed. My little sister had long red ringlets and petticoats. Our mother wouldn't let her play with us. She was supposed to be learning to be a lady. It wasn't fair, but we boys didn't care."

"Your sister?"

"Elizabeth. She died of diphtheria when she was ten."

This is the first I've heard of a sister. I'm having a hard time with the idea of Arthur swinging from a rope at a swimming hole; it's even harder to imagine his sister, doomed to an eternity of embroidery and watercolors.

"I'm sorry," I say. "I didn't know."

"There's a lot you don't know," he says. "I had an older brother too. Robert. Bobby. He was Mother's favorite. She didn't much care for me."

I totally get why she felt that way. "What happened to him?" I ask.

"Dead. Got bitten by a neighbor's rabid dog when he was thirteen. In those days there was no cure."

I don't know what to say. If Mom knows any of this, she has never told me.

"I'm sorry," I say again.

"Our father shot the dog. Almost shot the neighbor too. Would have if my mother hadn't stopped him." He gives a short bark of a laugh before he turns back to the TV. I wonder if he still misses them—Elizabeth and Bobby—or if most of the time it's as if they never existed. I don't know which is worse—forgetting your siblings or never having them in the first place.

That night, Mom freaks out when she sees my hair. Or lack of it. After years of telling me to get a haircut, she claims I've gone too far and that I look like a skinhead. A neo-Nazi. A thug.

"Mom, neo-Nazis don't usually wear orange Converse All-Stars and T-shirts that say *Lunenburg Folk Festival Volunteer.*"

"Even so, Rolly...Royce," she says. "You look different. Older." Like that's a bad thing.

"You should see Arthur," I mutter.

"What about him?"

"Uh, he's bald too. Balder than me. Totally shiny. Once you get used to it, it's kinda cool. Literally. His hat collection's coming in handy."

I laugh and Mom says, "You think this is funny? You're supposed to be looking after him, Royce, feeding him and keeping him clean and safe. Being responsible. Not letting him shave his head. What's next? Tattoos? Piercings?"

The minute she says it, I'm planning our next outing. Me and Arthur at the tattoo parlor. It's weird, the word *parlor*. The only time you ever hear it now is with the word *tattoo*, but I bet Arthur's sister had to sit in the stuffy parlor while Arthur sailed through the air at the swimming hole. I'm so stoked on the idea of getting tattoos on my bonking bumps—my initials, maybe?— that Mom has to yell at me to get my attention.

"Royce! Your grandfather has dementia, you know. Diminished capacity. His decision-making is compromised. Do you understand what that means?"

I nod. Diminished capacity for what? Sex? Probably, although he still talked a good game. Food? Yeah. Driving? Definitely. Walking? Yup. Personal hygiene? Undoubtedly. Cello-playing? For sure. But he wasn't dead yet. Not quite. He still had a huge capacity for leering, inappropriate touching, bad TV, ice cream, coffee, mockery and insult.

"Royce, are you paying attention to me?"

"Yup."

"How much did the cab cost?"

I am about to tell her I drove the T-bird, when I realize that she's in no mood to see it as a convenience rather than an illegality. I doubt whether she'll ever be in the mood. After all, I did search her room for Arthur's license, which, for all I know, has been revoked. I'll have to tell Arthur to keep the whole driving thing under his hat. Ha ha.

"Uh, yeah, the cab," I tell her. "Arthur has an account." To distract her I add, "You never told me about Elizabeth and Robert."

"Who?"

"Elizabeth and Robert. Your aunt and uncle."

"I don't have an aunt or an uncle," she says.

"Technically, no. But you could have. Arthur had a brother and a sister—they both died when they were kids."

Mom doesn't say anything right away. She gets up and starts loading the dishwasher. Her face is flushed and she is chewing her bottom lip, a sure sign she's upset. "He never talked about his childhood," she finally says. "I knew that his parents were born-again Christians, real Bible-thumpers, and that he grew up in a little town in Alberta, but that's about it." Her voice is flat, and I wonder if she's hurt that he confided in me and not her.

"I think the head-shaving triggered his memory," I say, as if that will somehow make her feel better. "His father used to shave Arthur's head in the summer. He didn't tell me much more. Just that his sister died of diphtheria; his brother died of rabies."

"I had no idea," she says. She sounds sad and tired and discouraged. Maybe the tattoos will have to wait.

Seven

The next morning, Arthur is still exhausted. I make him his *café au lait* as soon as I get there, but it sits in front of him, untouched, as he dozes in his high-back chair. When he wakes up, he is disoriented for a minute, and I can see the fear in his eyes. I don't think he knows who I am, but he knows he's at my mercy. I could do anything: Tie him up. Rob him. Kill him, even. The laptop alone must be worth some decent coin. Ditto the car. People have killed for less. The moment passes and he picks up the cup of coffee, takes a sip and roars, "Scum!"

For a second I think he's referring to me, and then I realize that the milky coffee has formed a scum while he slept. I'm with Arthur on that one. Scum is revolting. I move to take the cup away from him, but he hurls it on the floor before I can stop him.

"For fuck's sake, Arthur," I yelp as I jump out of the way. "I can make you a fresh one."

For a split second, he looks ashamed of himself, but then he rallies.

"Clean up the mess, boy, before it makes a stain. Do you know what this carpet is worth? Pure wool. Got it at an auction in 1960. Made by Persian toddlers. They sign them, you know. See, right down there in the corner. Little initials made by little fingers. Probably got paid ten cents for the whole damn thing."

I get a rag and a pail of warm water and get to work on the coffee stain. He's right about the initials. They're tiny, and next to them is what looks like a little bird. My eyes sting when I think of some poor little kid going blind making carpets for rich people. It's bad enough to be cleaning one.

"I bought my first cello at an auction," Arthur says as I scrub. "I was twelve. Never even heard a cello, let alone seen one. The only music I ever heard was the church choir."

He pauses to take a breath and then he sings, in a clear strong voice that sounds much younger than his usual rasp:

"I sing because I'm happy,
I sing because I'm free,
For His eye is on the sparrow,
And I know He watches me."

He stops singing, as suddenly as he started, and I wonder if he's forgotten the words or that he was telling me a story. His memory is selective, to say the least. I'm about to prompt him when he continues in his normal voice.

"At any rate, there was a country auction in our town—someone had died, I think, and the family was getting rid of a houseful of stuff. My father bought a pump organ for my mother. She played quite well. Learned when she was a girl in Ontario. I remember there was a crank gramophone, a baby carriage, a rifle and a cello. For some reason, I took the three dollars I had saved up from my chores and bid on the cello."

"Why the cello?" I ask from the floor, still scrubbing.

"Something about it appealed to me—the shape probably." He chortles. "Reminded me of my best friend's older sister. What I really wanted was the rifle, but Bobby outbid me. He died before he had a chance to use it though."

"How'd you learn to play?"

"I didn't touch it for a while. Just put it in my room in the corner. After Bobby died, I hauled it out to the backyard, took Bobby's shotgun and tried to add some holes to the cello." Arthur chortles. "I was a terrible shot. Maybe because I always closed my eyes at the last minute. So I dragged it back inside and tried to figure out how to play it. Drove my parents crazy, but pretty soon they were ordering me sheet music from Edmonton. Didn't have a proper lesson until I was fourteen. Then I spent a year un-learning all my bad habits."

I finish scrubbing and look up to see that Arthur is staring at his hands with tears streaming down his face. When he sees me watching him, he says, "What are you looking at, boy?" But his heart isn't in it. I push the box of tissues closer to him and take the pail of water into the kitchen. By the time I come back he has turned on the TV, and he doesn't even glance at me. I sweep the pile of snotty Kleenex into the wastebasket and head downstairs.

The first thing I do is check the car. Not that I think it will have gone anywhere. I just want to sit in it for a minute and stroke the steering wheel and inhale the vinyl smell. (Arthur told me that in 1956, vinyl was totally cutting edge. Way better than leather. Very space-age. Too bad if it made your ass sweat.) I wonder what it would be like to just open the garage door and drive away. I could be on the mainland in less than four hours, and the drive to Nova Scotia wouldn't take more than a week—maybe less if the weather was good all the way. I probably already have enough money to get across the country if I sleep in the car and eat at McDonald's. It's totally doable. Except for one thing: Mom. She doesn't deserve any of this. An ancient demanding father. An ungrateful runaway son. But then I didn't deserve to be wrenched away from my home and my friends either.

I get out of the car. The great escape will have to wait. I don't even have a change of clothes with me, let alone my iPod. In the absence of anything better to do, I decide to search for Arthur's cello. I figure it must be around somewhere. Not the one he bought when he was twelve, although that would be cool, but the one Mom has told me about. The insanely expensive one-of-a-kind instrument handmade by an Italian dude in the 1600s. Only the best for the great Arthur Jenkins.

Cellos are pretty big, and I figure this one will be in a hard case, which is about the size of your average nine-year-old. It doesn't take me long to search the downstairs. No luck. It's not hiding in a closet, or lying in wait under a bed or lurking behind a door. I continue my search upstairs, but the cello isn't wrapped up in one of Arthur's coats in the front hall closet. Nor is it sporting a rakish beret and smoking a Gauloise in the pantry off the kitchen. I grin at the idea of Arthur's cello chatting up a cute violin. When I get to Arthur's bedroom I have second thoughts about searching his room. It's an invasion of what little privacy he has left, and why am I trying to find the cello anyway? It's not like either of us can play it. But for some reason finding the cello seems important, so I persevere, even though the room smells really bad. While I'm in there, I strip the bed and throw the sheets by the door in case he wonders what I'm doing in his room.

I'm about to give up and go fix lunch when I spot something shoved in the back of his closet behind a box of old shoes. I get down on my hands and knees and move the box aside. There it is: a few hundred thousand dollars' worth of old wood. As I drag the cello case out into the light, Arthur rings the bell and yells for me. I consider shoving the cello back into the closet, but then I think, What the hell? and pick it up by its handle and head to the living room.

"Where's my lunch?" Arthur growls.

"Look what I found," I say.

I'm sure if Arthur was able to, he'd deck me, but he has to make do with turning purple and screaming, "Put that away! You have no right! I'll have the law on you!" Then he calls me a lot of names—miscreant, delinquent, bandit. He even calls me a dwarfish thief, which I happen to know is from *Macbeth*. It makes me laugh—being called dwarfish—which sets him off again. He pounds the desk until I start to worry that he's going to break the glass. Or have a heart attack.

"Okay, okay," I say. "I get it. You're upset. I'll put it back. Sorry for taking an interest." I turn to go back to his room and something hits me in the back. It hurts.

"Hey," I yell. "What are you doin', man?" His electric razor is lying on the floor beside me, and he is wheezing, not with rage but with laughter. Talk about mood swings.

"You should see your face, boy," he gasps. "What do they say in those ads? Priceless."

"Jesus, Arthur. That hurt."

"Pansy."

"Whatever," I say. "I'm going to put this away and then I'll make your lunch."

"Let me see it," he says.

"What?"

"Open it up."

"You sure?"

He nods.

I carry the case closer to him and stand it up where he can reach it. His hands are too stiff to undo the catches, and when I open the case, he makes no move to touch the instrument inside. He just stares at it, sighs and looks away.

I don't know what to say. It doesn't look much different from any other cello, but I know it is.

He reaches into the drawer of his desk, pulls out a flashlight and hands it to me.

"Take a look," he says.

"At what?"

"The signature."

"Uh, okay." I turn on the flashlight and wave the beam at the cello. I have no idea where someone would sign a cello.

"In there." He points at one of the F-shaped holes. "At the top."

I get down on my hands and knees and shine the light into the body of the cello. I can see what looks like spidery handwriting on a small, faded paper label—

letters and numbers. I can't make out what it says, but I don't have to.

"*Francesco Ruggieri detto,*" he says, "*il Per, Cremona, 1673.*"

I don't know how to speak Italian, but I can figure out what it means: Ruggieri made the cello in Cremona, Italy in 1673. "Cool," I say, even though the name doesn't mean anything to me. I've never seen anything that old though. "So, Frankie," I ask the cello, "what brings you to these parts?"

Arthur snorts. "Frankie."

I'm on a roll, so I continue the game.

"What's that you say, Frankie? You're a bit chilly? I can fix that."

I close the case and run to the hall closet. When I come back, I place one of Arthur's navy-blue berets on Frankie's hard head, and I wrap a long red scarf around his neck. I wish I had a Gauloise for him, but I guess smoking and three-hundred-and-fifty-year-old wood don't really go together.

"Maybe you could come for a ride with us sometime," I say to Frankie. "Arthur's car is awesome." I turn to Arthur. "Whaddaya say, Arthur? Should we show Frankie the town? Take him out for dinner? Go to a movie?"

"He's already seen Prague, New York, London, Berlin, Tokyo and Paris. What would he want with this rinky-dink place? Crumpets and tea?" Arthur swivels away from Frankie and grunts. "Is it lunchtime yet?"

"Sorry, Frankie. Duty calls," I say as I stand him up next to the piano and pretend to introduce them. "This is Wilhelmina Bosendorfer. You can call her Billy. She's a lot younger than you, so if you're anything like your owner, you should hit it off." I lift the cover off the piano's keys and run my fingers over the white keys. "Nice *glissando*, huh, Frankie?" I say with a leer. I don't play the piano, but you can't live with a piano teacher without picking up a few things.

"You should hear Frankie's *portamento*," Arthur says.

"What's a *portamento*?" I ask. "Sounds like a cross between a portmanteau and a pimento."

Arthur grunts. "You probably don't even know what a portmanteau is."

"Tanzania," I reply.

"Tanzania?"

"Tanganyika and Zanzibar. It's a portmanteau—you know—when two words blend to make a new word. Like brunch. Or Brangelina. Or mimsy. I'm not a complete dolt, you know."

"Mimsy?" Arthur says.

"You know, miserable and flimsy, as in 'All mimsy were the borogoves, and the mome raths outgrabe.' That's Lewis Carroll. Mom used to read it to me."

"I know who Lewis Carroll is, boy. *Alice in Wonderland*. *Through the Looking-Glass*. First books I ever read outside the Bible, my schoolbooks and the Eaton's catalogue in the outhouse. I went to school in Edmonton when I was fourteen, and someone had left a copy of *Alice* in my room at the boardinghouse. I read it from cover to cover the first week I was there. That was before anyone knew old Lewis was a bit of a pervert. Guess who my favorite character is."

I stare at him and try to remember the details of a book I haven't read in ten years. There are a lot of characters to choose from, and a lot of them are pretty wacky, as I recall. That old song comes into my head: *One pill makes you larger and one pill makes you small* and I remember my mom telling me that people used to think that Lewis was a bit of a stoner, the evidence being the hookah-smoking Caterpillar who advises Alice to eat the mushroom he's sitting on. I have no idea if Lewis was a perv or a stoner or both, but I'm pretty sure Arthur's favorite character isn't Alice or Humpty Dumpty or even the Mock Turtle. Then I've got it—the Red Queen. She and Arthur have a lot in common. Bad temper, paranoia, delusions of grandeur.

"Off with his head!" I yell, but he just frowns and shakes his head.

"Try again."

He's nuts, so I suggest the Mad Hatter.

He shakes his head again.

"The Cheshire Cat? Tweedle-dum? Tweedle-dee? The White Rabbit?"

He cackles after every suggestion and finally says, "Give up?"

I nod and he starts to recite "You Are Old, Father William," which has at least eight verses. He remembers every word, ending with a resounding *"Be off, or I'll kick you downstairs."* This from a man who couldn't tell you what he had for breakfast.

"Very impressive," I say. "I should have known your favorite character would be a cranky old man who can balance an eel on the end of his nose."

"Damn skippy," he replies.

Eight

Things settle into a comfortable, boring pattern over the next few weeks: I ride my bike to Arthur's every morning, he yells at me for being late or sweaty or stupid or all three, I open the curtains another inch, make him his *café au lait*, watch a bit of TV, make lunch, play some solitaire at the kitchen table, put his dinner in the microwave and ride home along the scenic route, which is longer but more interesting than the main roads. We take the T-bird out once a week and drive the same route I bike every day. Arthur often falls asleep in the car, like a fussy baby, and I drive around town until he wakes up and yells at me that he needs to go to the bathroom. If we were characters in a movie, Arthur and I would go on a road trip together and I would learn important life lessons from him and he would benefit from my *joie de vivre.* Like that's gonna happen. Even so, I cast the movie in my head: Arthur will be played by Kirk Douglas. The part of Royce Peterson will be played by Shia LaBeouf or maybe one of the *Twilight* dudes.

One day I drive all the way out to Sidney and back while he sleeps, just to see what it's like to drive the T-bird on the highway. It's amazing, but I'm glad to get back to town and let my blood pressure return to normal. If I hadn't had Arthur with me, I might have been tempted to continue past Sidney to the ferry terminal, slide up the ramp into the ferry's metal maw and be on my way.

One afternoon, sick of solitaire and really restless, I decide to look at Arthur's photo albums, which are decaying in the hall closet. I carry them to the unused upstairs bedroom, where I lay them on the bed and arrange them in chronological order. They start in 1929, when Arthur was fourteen, and go up to 2006. Nothing from his childhood in Alberta and nothing from the last four years. Each album covers a period of three to five years. Two albums are devoted to reviews and two are jammed with concert programs. They're all bound in dusty black leather, except for two small velvet-covered books—one blue, one red—labeled Marta and Nina. I place all but the first album on the bookcase. Then I make myself comfortable on the bed with 1929–1932.

The first thing I notice is that the dates on the cover are wrong: the first few pages are full of pictures of a pre-adolescent Arthur with an older boy and a younger girl. Bobby and Elizabeth. The girl has ringlets and a bow in her hair. She is also a little blurry, as if she can't keep still for the camera. In every photo, Arthur gazes adoringly at Bobby, who has a wide grin and freckles and often carries something: a rifle, a hoop, a dead gopher, a stick, a ball. In one picture, they are all standing outside what looks like a real teepee. In another, Arthur is in a small sled being pulled by a big dog. Happy childhood, right?

But a family portrait tells another story. A stern-looking man with a long beard stands with his hands clamped on the shoulders of a plump young woman, who is seated, holding a baby in a long white lace dress. The woman appears to have recently swallowed a mouthful of vinegar. Elizabeth is seated at the woman's feet, looking as if she is about to cry. The boys stand one on each side of their mother, hands clenched at their sides. No one is smiling. There might as well be a cross-stitched motto on the wall behind them: *Spare the rod and spoil the child*. I wonder what happened to the baby. Arthur only mentioned Bobby and Elizabeth. Maybe he has forgotten the baby's existence. For some reason, I find this really upsetting, to think that someone can evaporate like that.

A couple of blank pages follow the family portrait, and then it really is 1929. The scene shifts to a city that I assume is Edmonton. Arthur shoveling the sidewalk outside a run-down house. Arthur standing stiffly beside an elderly man in a fur-trimmed coat, a fur hat and leather gloves. Arthur is wearing hand-knitted mittens, a wool cap and a threadbare coat. He looks cold but happy. The old man has his hand on Arthur's elbow—he's either guiding him or leaning on him; it's impossible to tell which. Is he Arthur's cello teacher? A family friend? His landlord? A few pages later, I get my answer. A yellowing newspaper clipping dated 1931 features a photograph of the two of them. The caption under a photograph says: *Arthur Jenkins with his mentor and teacher Laszlo Polgar.* The headline reads: *Homegrown Prodigy Wins Prestigious Award.* The article goes on to say that Arthur has won a scholarship to study in London with a woman named Guilhermina Suggia. No one I've ever heard of, but what do I know? According to the article, she was a pretty big deal. She had a fling with Casals and she is described as "bohemian, unpredictable and temperamental." Just up Arthur's alley.

The rest of the album is devoted to pictures of Arthur in London. At first he looks bemused and hungry and a bit scared—he's really young to be so far from home— but by the time I turn the last page, he's got a tux, a car (an MG, I think) and a woman who could be the volatile (and much older) cello teacher. Things are looking up.

I'm about to move on to 1933–37 when the phone rings, which is weird. Arthur's phone hasn't rung once in all the time I've been here. If my mom wants to talk to me, she calls my cell, and no one ever calls for Arthur. Not when I'm here anyway. I wait to see whether Arthur is going to answer it, but when it keeps ringing I sprint to the living room and grab the phone off his desk. Arthur ignores it and me. He's watching *Little House* again and apparently the goings-on in Walnut Grove are pretty riveting.

"Hello," I say into the phone. "Jenkins residence."

"Is Arthur Jenkins there, please?" a woman's voice asks.

"May I say who's calling?" I ask. For some reason I think I need to screen Arthur's calls, or should I say, call.

"This is Catherine Ramm. I'm a producer with the CBC in Toronto. We're recording the concert soon, and I'd like to interview Mr. Jenkins for our pre-concert programming."

"What concert?" I ask. Arthur swivels in his chair and glares at me. He makes a throat-cutting gesture, which I take to mean that he doesn't want to talk to Ms. Ramm.

"The concert at Roy Thompson Hall. He's known about it for a year." She pauses. "To whom am I speaking?" Ms. Ramm is starting to sound a bit peeved, and Arthur is shaking his head so vigorously his tuque flies off.

"I am Mr. Jenkins' personal assistant," I say. "Royce Peterson. Mr. Jenkins is unavailable at the moment. I will have him return your call. Your number?"

Ms. Ramm sighs and rattles off a number, which I write down on a dirty napkin.

I hang up and say, "What concert, Arthur?"

Arthur is still glued to the TV; Mary is leaving Walnut Grove to go to a school for the blind. I reach over and swivel him around to face me.

"What concert?" I repeat.

He tries to turn back to the TV, but I've got a good grip on the back of the chair.

"Let go of me, boy," he growls.

"Nope," I say. "Not until you tell me about this concert."

"Damn people," he mutters.

"Who?"

"Promoters. Still trying to make a buck off an old man. There's a letter here somewhere. Let go of the damn chair, and I'll find it."

I let him turn the chair so he can get into his desk drawer. He pulls out a handful of mail, which he tosses at me. I sort through unopened bills, flyers for house-painters and requests for donations from three political parties, a public television station (as if) and a local homeless shelter. At the bottom of the pile is the letter from Catherine Ramm.

"Happy now?" he asks. "Bloodsuckers. Why don't they leave me alone?"

"Maybe because you were one of the greatest cellists of the twentieth century?"

He snorts and holds up his hands, which are shaking. The joints look swollen, his thumbs stick out at odd angles and his fingers are like claws. "The operative word in that sentence is *were*. You think I want people to see me like this?" He brandishes his hands at me. "Pathetic."

I'm not sure if he means he's pathetic or the people who want to honor him are, but the letter is very clear: There's going to be an all-star concert at Roy Thompson Hall to celebrate the airing of a CBC radio documentary on the life and times of my grandfather. The organizers are aware that Arthur can't travel, so they've arranged a gala event here at a fancy downtown hotel: white tie and tails, local celebrities, musicians, politicians. Which means speeches. And cameras. I wonder if any of the people putting this thing together has ever met Arthur. If they could see him now, glowering at the TV in his stained sweater and tattered slippers, they might think twice about the whole deal.

"Did you agree to go?" I ask.

"Maybe," he grunts, "a long time ago. That damn woman wouldn't let it go. I talked to her for hours, gave her names of people to talk to. You'd think they'd leave an old man in peace."

"What did you think—they'd forget about the guest of honor?"

He shrugs. "Who wants to see a smelly old man who can't play a note?"

"Well, I guess they do," I say, picking up the phone. "But I'll tell her you can't go to the party or do the interviews. I'm sure she'll understand. I mean—you *are* old."

Arthur darts out of his chair like a cobra from a snake-charmer's basket. He whips the phone out of my hand, sits down hard and hits *Redial.*

"I'll do the interviews next week," he tells the woman from CBC.

"Call my tailor," he says to me when he's off the phone. "We'll need new tuxes."

"We?"

"You and me, boy. And your mother will need a new dress. My treat. And tell her to have her nails done. Her hands are a disgrace."

That night I have dinner with my mother. After watching Arthur eat, it doesn't seem so bad to eat with someone who chews with her mouth closed, uses a napkin, rarely drools and doesn't call me "boy."

"You know about this concert thing?" I ask her over our pasta.

"Yes," she says. "But I didn't realize it was coming up so soon. They've been working on that documentary for years. Don't you remember them coming to the house in Lunenburg to interview me?"

I shake my head. In Nova Scotia I was always off with my friends, skateboarding, playing video games, riding my bike. I didn't pay too much attention to what my mom was doing as long as there was food in the fridge and hot water for long showers.

"Anyway," she continues, "the documentary should be good. I checked it all out before I let Arthur sign off on it. Lately I've been wondering if it was a mistake to say yes in the first place though. He was pretty angry with me for interfering, but I didn't want anyone to exploit him."

As if. She should be worried about Arthur exploiting them. Why does everyone treat him like his brain's as feeble as his body? I mean, yeah, sometimes the cogs slip, but most of the time he knows exactly what's going on. He just doesn't like it very much. I know how that feels.

"The documentary makers talked to a lot of people who knew him in his heyday," my mom is saying. "Apocalyptica is playing at the concert, at Arthur's request. Should blow the roof off Roy Thompson Hall!"

"Apocalyptica?" I say. "What's that?"

She cocks her head and smiles. "Wow. For once I know something you don't. Apocalyptica is a Finnish band that plays the music of Metallica and Slayer on cellos. Apparently they listened to Arthur a lot when they were classical music students in Helsinki, and they got in touch with him a while ago. Sent him some CDs. Now they're going to share the stage with a Chinese child prodigy and a string quartet from Italy. Should be fun, don't you think?"

I shake my head. "Arthur is a piece of work. First he refused to talk to the woman from CBC, and now he's setting up interviews and getting me to call his tailor."

"His tailor?"

"Yeah. New tuxes must be procured. And you need a new dress, apparently. His treat."

"A new dress?"

"And a manicure."

"Why?"

"'Cause I guess we're his dates, and we need to look good. Got a problem with that?"

She laughs and runs her hands through her hair. "Think he'd spring for a cut and color?"

"No problem," I say. "I am his trusted personal assistant, after all." I peek under the table at her feet. She's wearing gray woolen work socks and ancient Birkenstocks. "And get a pedicure while you're at it. And maybe some new shoes."

"You're a funny boy, Rolly," she says.

"That's Royce to you, ma'am."

Nine

A couple of days later, Arthur's phone rings again. This time it's a reporter from the local paper. She's heard about the upcoming concert and documentary, and she wants to interview the great Arthur Jenkins. There will be a photographer too.

"When would be a good time?" the reporter asks.

I want to laugh and say, "Never," but instead I take her number and promise to call her back when I've talked to Arthur, who yells at me for putting her off.

"You idiot," he roars. "Set it up for tomorrow."

To piss him off, I call her back and ask her to come in a week. Not that Arthur will remember when she's coming. Defying him just gives me a rare moment of satisfaction.

The day before the reporter and photographer are due, Arthur and I go back to Kim for a buzz and, in Arthur's case, a shave. After she's run the clippers over my head, I lie on the white leather couch, watching her apply hot towels to Arthur's face and wishing I could think of a good reason to ask her to shave me as well. Unfortunately, I've been stuck in fuzz mode since I was fifteen, and I only shave every few days, which is kind of okay, since shaving is a pain in the ass. If I ever do get some serious facial hair, I'll probably let it grow, just to see what happens. I'm not holding my breath though. Mom says Dad grew a mustache once, but it was made up of about ten long hairs. She made him shave it off.

Kim is doing her crooning thing again, and she kind of dances around as she works, singing snatches of the song that's playing on the sound system when she isn't telling Arthur to keep still and stop talking. Her ass is high and round and encased in some shimmery fabric that reflects the light from the spot lamps above her. It's kind of mesmerizing, like watching a disco ball when you're stoned, at least until Arthur roars, "Stop looking at her ass, boy, and get me a coffee."

I leap to my feet and run next door, catching a glimpse of my tomato-red head as I zip past one of the mirrors. Behind me, Arthur sniggers, and Kim tells him he's a naughty boy. By the time I come back with his coffee, she's removed the towels and is shaving him with long, slow strokes of a straight razor. His eyes are closed, and she gestures to me to put the coffee down on a side table.

"He's drifting off," she says. "Tomorrow's a big day for him."

I nod and take a sip of his coffee.

"He's fond of you, you know."

I snort and the latte goes up my nose. When I can speak again, I mutter, "You could have fooled me."

Kim stops shaving and points the razor at me. "And you're fond of him too."

I shake my head. "It's just a job. Good money. Believe me, there's no love lost."

"You're wrong," she says, returning to Arthur's face. "Dead wrong."

I shrug and pick up a *GQ* magazine to see if there are any tips on what to wear with a tux, but I can't stop thinking about what she said. I watch her wipe the shaving cream off Arthur's face. She sings, "*You're the top, you're the Coliseum. You're the top, you're the Louvre museum.*" When his face is clean, she massages his head in languorous circular motions.

When she gets to the end of the song, Arthur belts out, "*But if, baby, I'm the bottom, you're the top.*" I have to admit, at moments like this, yes, I'm fond of him. I laugh as Kim leans over and kisses Arthur on the cheek. "You got that right, honey," she says.

"You know it," he growls.

I roll my eyes and read an article on Bond girls while Arthur settles the bill and bids Kim goodbye. She gives me a hug as we leave. "Remember what I said," she whispers in my ear.

I nod dumbly, overwhelmed by the heat rising from her body, the smell of her perfume, the sticky touch of her lips against my ear. Then Arthur "accidentally" rams me with his walker, grins evilly and says, "Oops—sorry."

Right, Kim, I think. He's so fond of me.

When I get to Arthur's the next day, he's still in his room and he's in a foul mood. Big surprise. He's obviously flipping out about the interview, but he won't admit it. He's sitting on the bed in red long johns. The bed and the floor and every available surface are strewn with clothing.

"Where is it?" he snarls.

"Where is what?" I reply.

"You know what I mean. The suit. The Armani."

"You've got an Armani suit? Cool," I say. "And no, I didn't take it. Not much call for an Armani suit in my world, Arthur. And anyway, you're not my size."

"Then it must have been that maid, that Lily person. Probably took it and sold it."

I stick my head into the closet, which is almost empty except for a bunch of wire hangers, some ancient shoes and a dark heap in the farthest corner, behind where

I found Frankie. I crawl in and pull out the missing Armani, dusty and wrinkled, like its owner.

"You got a shirt to wear with this?" I ask.

Arthur shrugs and points at a pile by his bare feet. "Might be one in there."

I find a clean pale blue button-down shirt in the pile and take everything to the kitchen before I go in search of the ironing board and iron. Arthur follows me in his red long johns and sits at the kitchen table while I search the house. No ironing board. No iron. I'm about to stuff everything in my backpack and race home when he says, "In there, boy," and points at a narrow cupboard in the breakfast nook. I open it and find a built-in wooden ironing board with an iron on a recessed shelf behind it. Very ingenious. Arthur wheezes with laughter.

"You should have seen yourself, boy. Running all over the house."

"Jesus, Art," I mutter. "Do you have to be such a prick?"

At this point, I don't care if hears me. I'm not getting paid enough to put up with his shit. Actually, I am, but that's not the point. I've just spent half an hour turning the house upside down while he watched. It's possible he only just this second remembered where the ironing board was, but I doubt it. He's smiling as he pushes the walker over to his big chair and parks himself in front of the TV while I iron his suit. The iron doesn't have a Teflon coating or any steam vents; I put it on the Wool setting and hope for the best. When I apply the iron to the suit pants, it smells like the time I left my mittens on the woodstove when I was five. Almost burned the house down. But I still kind of like the smell. It reminds me of winter in Nova Scotia. Here on the West Coast it's all Gore-Tex and Polarfleece, which probably smells like burning tires when it catches fire.

I'm working on the shirt's cuffs, which are tricky, when Arthur yells, "Where's my coffee?"

"Cool your jets, Arthur," I yell back, wondering if this is how mothers feel when they're trying to get something done and their kids won't shut up. If so, why isn't there more infanticide? How does anyone stand the constant demands?

The interview is scheduled for eleven o'clock, which gives me two hours to make his coffee, get him cleaned up and put the suit on him.

I hang the shirt and suit on a wooden hanger, pick out some socks and a tie and make him his coffee. By the time I bring it to him, he's asleep in his chair, looking like a giant, ugly, bald baby in red sleepers. I cover him up with a plaid mohair blanket, and while he sleeps, I take the coffee to the extra bedroom and settle down on the bed with 1933–1937. When Arthur rings the bell half an hour later, I've drifted off with the album open to yet another picture of Arthur standing by yet another car with his arm around yet another woman. As far as

I can tell, from the age of about eighteen on, all Arthur did was play the cello, drive and fornicate. If the photos are any indication, he excelled at all three.

Getting him ready for the interview and photo shoot involves a lot of patience (on my part) and a great deal of swearing and flailing (on Arthur's part), but by the time the doorbell rings, he's back in his chair, looking clean, sane and almost handsome. If he'd lighten up a bit—lose the frown, try smiling—he'd actually look pretty good. I usher the reporter and photographer—both women— into the living room and a miracle takes place. Arthur stands up, unassisted, and makes his way around the desk to greet them. I notice that he's keeping one hand on the desk for support, but that doesn't stop him from kissing each woman's hand instead of shaking it. He's positively courtly as he invites them to sit down.

The reporter, a short, stocky middle-aged woman with heavy black glasses and straight gray hair, drags a kitchen chair up to the desk, takes out a small tape recorder and sets it on the desk. She pulls a laptop out of her bag and sets it up as the photographer, who is younger and a whole lot hotter, wanders around the room, looking a bit bemused. Or maybe she's just trying to figure out the best angle to shoot Arthur from. It's definitely a challenge. When she catches me staring at her ass, she smiles and mimes taking my picture as the dreaded blush stains my cheeks.

"*Café au lait,* ladies?" Arthur asks as he creeps back to his chair. "It's absolutely no trouble at all. Royce here is at your command."

He waves his hand at me, and they both smile and nod.

"Three *cafés au lait,* coming up," I say. I catch Arthur's eye as I turn to leave the room. He winks and gives a tiny shrug, as if to say, "What can you do?"

When I come back with the coffee, Arthur is talking, and he doesn't stop for about an hour. The reporter asks a few questions, but mostly she just lets Arthur ramble while she taps away at her laptop. The funny thing is, Arthur almost seems to be interviewing her. By the time he says he's too tired to continue, he's found out that the reporter's nickname is Midge, she has two grown children (one in rehab, one a lawyer), she's divorced and she loves dachshunds. I'm not sure how this happens (I'm distracted by the photographer's stiletto boots and the fact that when she squats I get a glimpse of the tattoo on her lower back: it looks like a swordfish or maybe a narwhal), but by the time Midge shuts off the tape recorder, she and Arthur are acting like old friends.

The photographer, whose name is Bettina, asks Arthur to come and sit by the window to be photographed. As he heaves himself up and shuffles over to the chair she has positioned for him, she yanks the curtains open—all the way. I expect Arthur to freak, but he doesn't say a word, just lowers himself into the chair and stares out to sea as Bettina snaps, fusses with the camera and snaps some more. Arthur sits patiently, talking to Midge in between shots.

"Beautiful woman, my first wife," he says. "Met her in Budapest just after the war. Voice of an angel. We came back to Canada together, but she never stopped missing her family. Her country. She died giving birth to Marta. I didn't know what to do."

Tears form in his eyes, and Midge reaches over and pats his hand. I want to say, "He let other people raise her—that's what he did," but I keep my mouth shut. I realize I'm not actually sure who looked after Aunt Marta, but I doubt it was Arthur. So I'm blown away by what he says next.

"I took a year off the concert circuit after Marta was born," Arthur says, as if in reply to my unspoken comment. "But I needed to be earning money, so I hired a nanny to travel with me and look after Marta. When Marta was five, I bought a house in Toronto, and the nanny, Coralee, moved into it with Marta. I came home as often as I could, but I didn't see Marta as much as I should have. I know that. Coralee and I got married in 1958, but once Marta went off to university, we divorced. I was never home, and Coralee wanted a child of her own. Haven't seen her in years. She must be almost eighty now. An old lady. And Marta…she says she doesn't even remember the years of touring with me. All she remembers is her private school and Coralee."

"I'm sure you did your best," Midge says. I stifle a snort. Arthur nods solemnly. Bettina keeps snapping.

Arthur's eyes start to droop, and suddenly I want to get these women out of the house. I want Arthur back in his old clothes, sitting at his desk watching *Little House*. I want to go back to the photo albums and find pictures of Aunt Marta and Coralee.

"He's toast," I say. "I mean, I think he's done as much as he can."

Midge and Bettina nod and start to collect their things as I help Arthur back to his chair behind the desk. Before they leave, Midge and Bettina crouch down, one on each side of Arthur (allowing me a closer look at the tattoo—definitely a narwhal) and thank him for his time, for his generosity, for his story. He smiles as they kiss his papery cheeks.

"I'm going to write a book, you know," he says, his voice low and slow. "The story of my life." He taps his bald head. "It's all up here. Every bit of it. Haven't forgotten a thing."

Midge nods and puts her business card on his desk. "If you ever need any help…," she says.

"That's what I've got him for," Arthur says, pointing at me. "Him and a MacBook." He chortles at the look on my face, which must be a combination of surprise, dismay and grudging admiration. I remember the empty file named *Me*. He's totally conned Midge and Bettina into thinking he's a great human being, and now he thinks he's going to con me into helping him write the fantasy version of his life and times. No way. I didn't sign on to be a ghostwriter. Just a babysitter.

Ten

The day after the interview, Arthur and I drive to his tailor to get fitted for our tuxes. The shop is basically two rooms on the main floor of a shabby old house in Oak Bay. The front room is the showroom and fitting room. Floor-to-ceiling shelves hold bolts of fabric, and a bunch of well-dressed, blank-faced mannequins stand at attention along the back wall. The back room is a workroom, full of sewing machines, cutting tables, ironing boards and half-constructed suits. There is no sign outside, no cash register, no overhead lighting, no sales associates, no mood music. Just one ancient gnome-like man in a dusty suit with a tape measure and a piece of tailor's chalk, and three silent old guys in the back room, hunched over their work. I half expect Tiny Tim to pop out and say, "God bless us, every one."

"Mr. Wadsworth and I go way back," Arthur says as I ease him into a wingback chair, the only furniture in the room. "He used to make suits for British royalty, isn't that right, Ben?"

Mr. Wadsworth nods gravely. "Long time ago, Mr. Jenkins. Long time ago. Savile Row, it was. Been here for almost fifty years now."

"Ben followed his heart. Didn't you, Ben?" Arthur says. "Married a Canadian nurse after the war. She wanted to come home, so he came with her."

Mr. Wadsworth smiles. "And I'd do it again," he says to me. "Yes, I'd certainly do it again. Got away from all that pomp and circumstance, didn't I? No royalty here, just good fellows like your grandfather. Always a need for a beautiful bespoke suit, even in the colonies."

He wheezes out a laugh and advances toward me with his tape measure, a little cloud of chalk dust following in his wake, like Charlie Brown's friend Pigpen.

"Bespoke?" It sounds like something to do with bicycles, which can't be right.

"Made to measure, my boy. Made to measure."

"Oh."

"Stand still, stand still," he says as he wraps the tape measure around my neck. I gag a little, and he mutters, "Sorry, sorry," and moves on to my chest. After each measurement he says a number twice before he moves on to the next measurement. Waist, shoulders, arms, hips, inseam (gross), crotch (even grosser), outside leg, thigh, knee, ankle. There may have been more, but he goes so fast I can't keep track. When he's done, he asks me my age, weight, height and whether I am right- or left-handed, repeating every answer twice after I say it. Then he scurries into the back room and reappears a few minutes later with a notebook open to an amazing sketch of me—front and rear views—with all my measurements in all the proper places. I swear it takes him less than five minutes and it even looks like me. Me in a single-breasted tuxedo, that is.

"Black shirt or white, young sir?" he asks.

"Black?" I say. I've seen guys at the Oscars doing the black-on-black thing and it looks pretty cool, especially with a shaved head.

"Excellent choice. Excellent choice. Flat front or pleats?" He gestures at the pants.

"Flat front. Definitely flat front." Even I know pleats are for geeks and old men.

"Very good. Very good. Double vents or single?" This time he points to the back of the jacket.

"Single, I think. More streamlined, right?" I'm kind of getting into it now, imagining what I'll look like in my bespoke tux. A young James Bond? A total asshole? It could go either way.

"Yes, yes, quite right. And peak lapels on the jacket, I think. Yes, peak lapels."

I have no idea what peak lapels are, but I figure Mr. W. knows what he's doing.

"And what about one of those?" I ask, pointing at one of the mannequins, which is sporting a blood-red vest.

Mr. Wadsworth glances at Arthur, who nods.

"A waistcoat. Splendid." Mr. Wadsworth smiles and pats my arm, leaving a perfect imprint of his hand. "Perfectly splendid. Silk and wool blend for the suits, Mr. Arthur?" Mr. W. scuttles over to the wall of fabric, scrambles nimbly up a wooden ladder, grabs a bolt of material, clambers down and drapes the fabric over Arthur's lap. He's kind of like one of Santa's elves on crack. Arthur caresses the fabric as if it's a woman's hair and nods his approval again.

Mr. W. rubs his hands together and coughs when he inhales the resulting flurry of chalk dust.

"Your turn, Mr. Arthur," Mr. W. announces. He goes through the same measuring process with Arthur, producing an eerily accurate drawing in less time than it takes to take a leak.

Arthur decides on a white shirt, pleat-front pants and no waistcoat. I choose patent leather dress shoes, but Arthur declines shoes, mumbling something about his bunions. We make an appointment to come back for a fitting; Mr. W. promises that the tuxes will be ready in plenty of time for the gala event. "We'll put you to the front of the line, Mr. Arthur," he says. "Front of the line."

We're almost home when Arthur says, "Where did you get those shoes?"

"Which shoes?"

"The ones you're wearing."

"These?" I lift my foot off the gas. I'm wearing red Adidas, but I can't imagine why he cares where I bought them.

"Uh, downtown," I reply. "At a store downtown."

"Take me there," he commands.

"Why?"

"I want some to wear with my tux."

"You want Adidas? For your tux?" I turn toward downtown, wondering if this is the dementia talking or what.

"I want to be comfortable. And stylin'."

"Stylin', Arthur?" He really is watching too much MTV.

"Just drive," he growls.

It's pretty weird taking your ninety-five-year-old grandfather into a store that caters to dudes in baggy low-rise jeans, vintage track jackets and unlaced skate shoes, but Arthur's all over it. Gone is the bloody-minded crank I have to put up with. In his place is a sprightly old hipster, oozing charm and good will. Within five minutes, he's got the owner fitting him for shoes and another guy showing him funky T-shirts, while I skulk behind a display of Baby Phat jeans and enormous rhinestone-encrusted handbags. By the time we leave, he has two new pairs of shoes (yellow Adidas and black and white Puma hightops), a Stussy camo hoodie, a pair of Oakley sunglasses and two new friends whom he's invited to the gala.

"Dress up," he advises them as we leave. "No baggy jeans, no camo, no obscene T-shirts."

They nod and smile like bobble-head dolls. Really cool bobble-head dolls in three-hundred-dollar kicks.

"See you later, dude," they chorus. One of them gives Arthur a fist bump which almost knocks him over.

"Nice boys," Arthur says as we drive away.

The closer the gala gets, the grumpier Arthur becomes. When we go for our final tux fittings, he complains about everything: the cost (too high), the fit of his pants (too tight), the temperature in the shop (too low). Mr. W. is patient, but I can tell he's happy when we leave. The gala is on a Sunday, and the plan is for Mom to get Arthur ready for his big evening. We have to be at the hotel by seven, so Mom's supposed to come home around five to do whatever it is she needs to do before she goes out. A limo will pick Arthur up at six fifteen and then swing by for us. Simple enough, except that Mom phones me at three o'clock and tells me that Arthur has barricaded himself in his room. Whenever she tries to get him to let her in, he bellows, "Send the boy."

"Can you come over?" she asks.

"Jeez, Mom. What for?" I ask. "He'll just yell at me too. Or throw shit at me. No thanks. He'll get over it. Anyway, I was just going out."

"Where?"

"Car dealership."

"Oh, Rolly," she sighs. "Couldn't it wait?"

I'm actually not even dressed, and I haven't done much all day other than sleep and eat and watch TV. I thought about checking my Facebook page, but I'm not sure I want to know what my buddies back home are doing. Probably not hanging out with demented old men, that's for sure. My friends and I used to joke about getting out of Lunenburg right after high school. Going to the big city—Halifax or Toronto or Vancouver. They probably think I'm lucky—I got out early. I try to imagine what I would say if I wrote to anyone now.

Hey, I'm babysitting my grandpa for the summer. I had mono so I'm not going to school. I shaved my head. I'm getting a bespoke tux. Your buddy, Royce.

For all I know, they've forgotten my existence. What's that saying? Out of sight, out of mind. I have no hard evidence that absence makes the heart grow fonder. When I first got to Victoria, I talked to my buds a lot, spent a lot of time on Facebook, but as time went on it sort of withered away—on both sides. I had nothing to say, and I didn't want to hear about the latest camping trip or how one of them had scored with Peaches.

I sigh and tell Mom I'll be over as soon as I can.

When I get to Arthur's house, Mom is sitting on the deck staring out to sea. There's no actual furniture on the deck, so she's just sitting cross-legged, with her back against the house. I sit down next to her and she says, "This is ridiculous."

I nudge her a little bit with my shoulder. "Yup."

She nudges me back and says, "What's wrong with me?"

"Uh, Mom? It's not you. He's nuts. You're fine." She starts to speak, but I cut her off. "Yeah, I know. He's not, like, certifiable or anything, but for practical purposes— for our purposes—it's easier to just think of him as nuts. That's what I do. Keeps the expectations low. In five minutes he'll probably be telling me to go away and begging you to come back."

I get up and pull her to her feet.

"But why today, Rolly? His big day. All I was doing was trying to help him get dressed."

I shrug. "Who knows? Maybe he's scared."

"Scared? Arthur? He loves being the center of attention. He's made a career out of being the center of attention."

"Yeah, but..."

"But what? You think you know him better after spending a few weeks with him?" Mom stomps into the kitchen and grabs her purse and keys. "Fill your boots," she says as she heads for the door. "I'm getting my hair done; then I'm going home for a bubble bath and a glass of wine. See you later."

The front door slams and I hear the truck start. It's not like Mom to freak out, and I wonder what Arthur said to her, what button he pushed. There's no sound from his room, and I'm tempted to let him stew for a while, but it's getting late. I need to get him organized so I can go home and get ready myself.

I bang on his door and yell, "Open up!" The door swings away at my touch and reveals Arthur in his black Jockey shorts, sitting on the edge of his bed.

"It's about time," he says. "Your mother's useless. Always has been."

Suddenly I'm tired of being levelheaded Royce. The good kid. The obedient son. I hate looking after Arthur. Right now, I hate Arthur.

"You're an asshole," I say. "Just so we're clear. I'm here to help you get ready, but I'm not listening to any more of your shit. Not about Mom. Not about me. People try to help you, you know? And what do you do? You insult them and mock them and make their lives a living hell. Why? Because you're the great Arthur Jenkins? Because you feel sorry for yourself and you want everyone to feel as bad as you do?" My heart's pounding, and my hands clench into fists. I want so much to punch him, but what satisfaction would there be in decking someone who can't stand up without assistance? That would just make me a bully and an elder abuser, or whatever it's called.

"How dare you," Arthur growls.

"How dare I what? Call you on your shit? Oh, I dunno. Maybe it's because you constantly trash my mom when she tries to help you. Maybe it's because you call me boy instead of Royce. Maybe it's because I'm pissed that my dad died when he was twenty-six, and I never got a chance to know him. Maybe it's because it's not fair that he's dead and you're alive. Maybe it's because I hate living here. Pick one." I'm breathing hard, the way I do after riding up a hill, and Arthur is staring down at his lap. I can see his ribs rising and falling; his skin is pale and saggy and flaky, like an albino elephant with psoriasis. It looks like he's had a shower—a wet towel is on the floor by the bed—but that's as far as he got.

As I lean over to pick up the towel, he looks up at me, winks and mutters, "Congratulations on growing a pair."

I'm not sure how to respond—it would be weird to say "Thank you"—so I don't say anything, and he doesn't pursue it. Hard to believe that he likes it that I called him an asshole, but I have to admit that it felt good to ream him out. Really good. I pull the garment bag out of the closet, unzip it and lay the tux out on the end of the bed.

I'm about to start putting on his shirt when he says, "Black silk socks. In the top drawer."

I rummage around until I find them and drop them on the floor by his feet. I notice the nails on one foot are long; on the other they are trimmed but ragged. The clippers lie on the floor by his feet. Maybe that's what set him off—trying to trim his own nails. I don't care. I'm not trimming his nails, and I'm not feeling sorry for him.

He doesn't say another word while I dress him and neither do I. We communicate by hand gestures, right down to the cufflinks and the shoes (he's wearing the black and white Pumas). If I wasn't so pissed with him, I'd tell him how awesome he looks, but instead I lead him to the kitchen table, tie a towel around his neck and give him his dinner. When he's done, I help him back to his desk chair and get ready to go. The curtains are wide-open, which is weird, but I leave them alone, even when Arthur turns on the TV. If he wants my help, he can ask for it. Nicely.

"See you later," I say. "The limo'll be here for you at six fifteen. Don't forget to pee first."

"I'm not six," he says.

"Might as well be," I say under my breath.

The tux isn't the most comfortable thing I've ever worn, but it's definitely the most expensive. And the most flattering. I was afraid the patent leather shoes would look a bit, uh, effeminate, but they rock, as does the black shirt and the burgundy waistcoat. I run my hand over my nonexistent hair, check my nose for boogers and I'm good to go. Mom, on the other hand, is still fussing around in her room when the limo driver comes to the door. His eyes bug out when he sees her. She's wearing a tight black knee-length halter-top dress, high-heeled black shoes, dangly earrings and a sparkly red shawl. She pats her hair, which is long and full and wavy. Her fingernails are bright red.

"Extensions." She giggles. "Who knew? And look at you. My little boy...all grown up." I bow, and she giggles again.

The limo driver clears his throat, and Mom blushes. I offer her my arm as we go out. The limo is huge and we sit facing Arthur, who is huddled in a corner, looking miserable. No one speaks as we drive to the hotel. When we get there, everything changes. Suddenly Arthur is the life of the party, and Mom is whisked away by a woman who is already a little bit drunk and a whole lot silly. Me? I stand behind a potted palm and watch the show, which is mostly well-dressed people getting drunk on free booze and listening to a bunch of speeches about how great Arthur is. The guys from the clothing store turn up wearing suits and shades and a lot of bling. No camo. No baggy pants.

I'm thinking about going over to talk to them when one of the catering staff, a really cute girl whose name tag says *Dani*, comes up to me with a tray of appetizers and says, "I know you. You're in my math class. Or you used to be. There was a rumor going around that you were in jail."

Jail? Talk about an undeserved reputation. I will myself not to blush as I answer her. "I had mono."

"Oh, yeah? My friend had that. Totally sucks. When you coming back?"

"Um, I don't know. September, I guess."

"What are you doing here?" she asks.

I take one of the appetizers off the tray, hoping to keep her with me a few minutes longer. I point to Arthur, who's surrounded by laughing women. "He's my grandfather."

"You're kidding me. He's, like, ancient. Way older than my grandpa."

"Yup." I grab a shrimp roll and stuff it in my mouth. "He's ninety-five."

She smiles as she stares at Arthur, who is now sitting in a wingback chair with a martini in one hand, holding court. "Sweet shoes. He's sort of cute, for an old guy. Must run in the family." She looks straight at me, her brown eyes bright, and this time the blush rises to my cheeks.

"Awww, that's so sweet," she says, putting down the tray and whipping a pen out of her apron pocket. She writes a number on my palm, which I pray isn't sweaty. "Call me. We should hang out."

I watch her ass swaying in her short black skirt as she walks away. I can't believe it. A hot girl just came on to me at Arthur's party, and there's no one to tell. Not my mom, that's for sure, although it looks as if at least one guy is hitting on her. Then the guest of honor breaks away from his harem and makes his way slowly toward me, a girl on each arm. He looks like a really ancient, wizened Hugh Hefner. He's grinning at me, and I realize there is at least one person I can tell.

Eleven

The morning after the party, Mom sleeps in. Or to be more accurate, she stays in her room with a bucket beside the bed and the curtains drawn. I stick my head in to say goodbye before I leave for Arthur's, but all she does is groan and pull the pillow over her face. Her black dress is on the floor, crumpled beside the sparkly shawl. I wonder if I'm going to find a similar scene at Arthur's, although I don't think he was drunk the night before, just happy. He fell asleep in the limo on the way home, and I had to undress him, get him to the bathroom and tuck him in while Mom entertained the limo driver by playing show tunes on the grand piano. By the time I got Arthur settled, she and the driver were singing a duet of "Some Enchanted Evening."

When I open the door at Arthur's, the first thing I notice is a breeze coming from the living room. Now, the one thing I know for sure is that Arthur can't stand drafts. It can be eighty degrees and humid, but if he feels a breeze, he goes on a mission to find its origin and eliminate it. He wears long johns year-round. So there's no way he's opened the door to the deck to let some fresh air into the house. I start to run, wondering if there's been a home invasion, and if so, whether the MacBook is gone. Or the car. I'm momentarily ashamed that my first concern hasn't been for Arthur, who might be bleeding to death on the Persian carpet. But he's not there. Or in his chair. A dish of ice cream is melting on his desk, the TV is on and the door to the deck is open. Arthur is on the deck, lying in a heap beside an overturned chair and a bucket of water. He's dressed in his bathrobe, and a damp cloth is clutched in his hand. He's hasn't been bludgeoned or robbed, but instead of feeling relieved, I feel angry. I don't need this. Neither does Mom. He's done something stupid, and we'll have to deal with it. Like always.

His eyes flutter open as he tries to raise his head off the deck.

"What the fuck, Arthur," I say. "Lie down. I'm calling an ambulance." I pull my cell phone out of my pack and dial 9-1-1 while I run into the house for a pillow and blanket.

"What is the nature of your emergency?" the 9-1-1 operator asks. The nature, I think. The nature is... what are the choices? Stupidity, arrogance, senility, pigheadedness?

"Police, fire or ambulance," she prompts.

"Ambulance. He's fallen. My grandfather. He's conscious, I think. Or he was a minute ago."

She transfers me to someone else who takes my name and the address, and I go back out to the deck and slide a pillow under Arthur's head and cover him with the blanket. He is very pale, and even though I don't really know what I'm doing, I take his pulse, just to feel like I'm in control. It's racing, so I check my own, for comparison. My pulse is also very fast. I have no idea what this means, although I can't imagine it's a good thing. His skin is cold and sweaty, which strikes me as an odd combination. There's a bump the size of a Ping-Pong ball on the back of his head. It's bleeding a bit, but I don't touch it.

"The windows...," he mutters. "Filthy." He's slurring his words like he's drunk, but I know he isn't.

"You were trying to clean the windows? What are you—insane?"

He nods and then winces. "I'm cold, Rolly," he whispers. "Take me inside." Thank god I've watched a lot of TV: at least I know better than to move him. I get some more blankets and settle myself beside him to wait for the paramedics, who take their sweet time getting there.

Or that's what it feels like anyway. When the siren whoops to a stop outside the house, I let go of Arthur's hand, which I hadn't even realized I was holding, and run to open the door. The paramedics, a woman and a man, are gentle and patient with Arthur, even when he rallies a bit and tells them to go to hell.

"No hospital," he wails.

"'Fraid so, old son," the male paramedic says. "That's a nasty bump you've got. Need to have it checked out."

"Anyone you can call?" the woman asks me. "Someone who can sign him in at the hospital?"

"Call?"

"An adult? Next of kin?"

"I'm his grandson. I'll go with him."

"How old are you?"

"Sixteen. Almost seventeen."

She shakes her head. "Sorry. You can ride with him, but we really need an adult at the hospital."

"I'll call my mom." She nods and goes to help strap Arthur onto a stretcher. He's protesting, but weakly, as we make our way out to the ambulance. Mom's not picking up her cell—it's probably turned off—so I call the home number over and over until she picks up.

She sounds like she's got a mouthful of cotton balls. "Rolly...wha—?"

"Arthur fell. I called an ambulance. We're on our way to the hospital. They need an adult and..."

"Is he okay?" she asks. I imagine her sitting up in bed, clutching her head, trying to stop the bile from rising into her throat.

"I don't know. I think so, but they say he needs to be checked out. I didn't know what to do, Mom."

"It's okay, Royce. You called nine-one-one. That's the important thing."

"I guess." And I did get him pillows and a blanket. "The ambulance is leaving, Mom. Will you be at the hospital?"

"I'm on my way," she says. All traces of the giggly, tipsy woman of the night before are gone. Arthur strikes again.

At the hospital we spend hours at Emergency, waiting with Arthur in a hallway with about ten other people on gurneys. Apparently the ER is full, and Arthur's injuries aren't bad enough to get him in right away. With every passing minute, he gets more lucid and more verbal. When he finally needs to take a leak, things get nasty.

"You'll just have to use this, Mr. Jenkins. I can't let you get up." A nurse in a pink-flowered smock hands Arthur a gourd-shaped blue plastic jug which he smacks out of her hand. It makes a lot of noise as it skitters down the hall. At least it wasn't full. Everyone is staring at us, but Arthur doesn't care. He sits up, swinging his bony white legs over the edge of the gurney. Mom and I grab him before he tries to jump off.

"Dad, please," Mom says as we wrestle him down. "You can't get up."

"I'm not taking a piss out here," he roars.

The nurse reappears with another blue jug that she thrusts at Mom.

"Here's another urinal," she says. "That's the best I can do. We'll try to get him in soon."

"Try harder," Mom snaps. She turns to Arthur, who is glaring at us, but immobile.

He grabs the urinal, flings the sheet back, pulls up his hospital gown, sticks his dick into the mouth of the urinal and lies back on his pillows as the stench of his piss fills the corridor. Mom gasps and whips the sheet over him, but not quickly enough. "Disgusting!" "Sonofabitch!" "Nurse!" "Put that thing away!" The corridor rings with the sound of outrage. One old lady sits up suddenly and cries, "Where? Where?" Arthur closes his eyes and smiles as a different nurse appears and wheels him into the ER, pulls a curtain around him and takes away the urinal.

"Shame on you," she says, but she's obviously not particularly upset. I guess Arthur's dick doesn't rate very high on the grand scale of Emergency-room grossness. Arthur shrugs, as if to say, "What can you do?" and I swear she winks at him. What's up with that? He's just exposed himself in a public space, and the nurse is acting like he's adorable.

Five hours later, Arthur is finally admitted for overnight observation, and the mystery of the winking nurse is solved: she's been a big fan of Arthur's since the days when she played the cello in the National Youth Orchestra. By the time Arthur is settled in his room, Mom and I are exhausted. We don't talk much on the ride home. When we get there, we go to our rooms and sleep. I don't think I've ever been so tired, even when I had mono.

When I get up, it's getting dark and Mom is sitting at the kitchen table in a baggy T-shirt and shorts, drinking tea and talking on the phone.

"The doctors say it was likely something called a TIA. A Transient Ischemic Attack. A mini-stroke. Maybe not the first."

I grab a Diet Coke from the fridge and sit down at the table. Mom mouths "Marta" at me and says, "Uh-huh. Uh-huh. He's being seen by a specialist tomorrow. No, I don't think they're doing an MRI. He's feeling pretty good now. They just want to watch him overnight. He would have left today if they'd let him. You know Arthur."

Mom rolls her eyes and puts the phone on Speaker. Marta's shrill voice fills the room.

"Is he getting the best doctors, Nina? And a private room? He can afford it, you know."

"I know," Mom says. "There just aren't any available right now."

"Oh, now, Nina. Surely that's not true. You just have to be more assertive. What's the hospital's number?

I'll get Horst to call. You know how forceful he can be. Do they even realize who Arthur is?"

Mom snorts green tea out her nose, and I pipe up, "Oh, yeah. They know."

"Rolly, is that you? Are you helping your mother? You're the man of the house, you know. That's what I always say to Horst. 'Rolly's the man of the house now.'"

"Bad connection, Aunt Marta," I say. "I can hardly hear you. We'll have to call you back." I press the End button and look over at Mom.

"Talk about forceful," she says. "Thanks, man of the house."

"You're welcome. Is there anything to eat?"

The hospital calls the next day and tells us to come and get Arthur. All his vital signs are good, so I offer to bring him home if Mom will drop me off at the hospital and give me money for a cab. She's more than happy to fork over twenty bucks and head off to a landscaping job. I wish I could take the T-bird, but Mom still doesn't know Arthur lets me drive it, and I don't think this is the time to tell her. When I get to the hospital, he's sitting by the elevator in a wheelchair. He's wearing his bathrobe, and I realize he doesn't have any other clothes. On his feet are some green paper booties, but he doesn't seem to care.

"Get me out of here."

"Nice to see you too, Arthur." I wheel him down to the front doors, where a cab is waiting. When we get to his house and I help him in, he collapses into his chair, orders me to get him some ice cream and falls asleep before I can bring it to him. The curtains are still wide-open, and the chair and bucket he was using are still lying on the deck. He's right. The windows are filthy. I fill the pail with soapy water, add a little vinegar and get to work. The sun is shining. A hot girl gave me her phone number. Arthur is asleep. I feel happier than I have since we moved here. I hum as I scrub the glass. Maybe the worst is over. For me. For Mom. For Arthur.

I couldn't have been more wrong. Arthur has three TIAs in less than three weeks and ends up in the hospital twice, lying for hours in the ER, waiting to be examined and discharged. By now I know the warning signs: dizziness, slurred speech, disorientation and an intense desire for ice cream, preferably chocolate. The third time it happens, in late July, instead of calling 9-1-1 right away, I help him into bed and check him every hour or so, which is all they ever do at the ER anyway. Going to the ER again isn't part of my plan.

I'm meeting Dani, the girl from Arthur's party, later. We're going for a bike ride and maybe to the beach. I called her the week after the gala, and we've hung out a couple of times. I really like her, even though she's better than me at a lot of things. Most things, really. School, sports, music. She's not perfect though. For instance, she has an irrational fear of bugs—all bugs. Even ladybugs, if you can believe it. And butterflies. And she's kind of impatient sometimes. You don't want to be waiting in a lineup with her. She sighs and fidgets and rolls her eyes. She also hates vanilla ice cream and hockey. But that's about the worst of it. Anyway, going for a bike ride is the next step toward a real date, so no way do I want to be stuck at the hospital, waiting for Mom to get off work. I'm sure Arthur will be okay. He always is.

Because I need to be able to hear Arthur if he calls, I spend the day in the second bedroom, going though the photo albums. I'm looking at some pictures of Aunt Marta when she was a little girl when I hear him yell, "No!" He sounds more surprised than upset, so I figure he must be talking in his sleep and I go back to the photo album. I've reached the Coralee years and I wonder why Aunt Marta never talks about her. Maybe Marta can't forgive her for disappearing, if that's really what she did. You'd get kind of a complex, I guess, if first your mother died and then your stepmother abandoned you.

When I get up to check on Arthur again, it's almost time for me to meet Dani, but it doesn't seem right to leave him alone. He's pretty out of it. I text her and tell her I might have to bail on the bike ride. I hope she isn't pissed. My limited experience with girls is a) they hate being stood up, and b) they always assume guys are lying, even when they have no evidence. Nothing I can do about that now. Dani hardly knows me. I've told her about Arthur, but not in any detail. Don't want to scare her off. I step into Arthur's room and I can tell right away that something is really wrong. He is gray and sweaty again, and one side of his face is twisted into a grimace. He opens one eye as I approach the bed. One hand reaches for me and pulls me down close to his face. When he speaks, his voice is so hoarse and slurred I can't make out the words. I'm pretty sure he's had another stroke— a big one this time. The one all the doctors warned us about. If he dies, I might as well have murdered him. If I'd called 9-1-1 earlier in the day, he would have been at the hospital when the big one happened. They might have been able to prevent it. It's my fault. All because I wanted to go for a bike ride with a girl. I stand beside him, my mouth suddenly dry, my hands sweaty. What was it he'd said? *I'd be better off dead.* Did he really mean it? If he really wanted to die, would calling 9-1-1 now be wrong? And wouldn't we *all* be better off if he was dead? I shudder and fumble in my pocket for my phone.

"It's gonna be okay, Arthur. I'm gonna call Nina. It's gonna be okay."

He groans as I call 9-1-1 and then Mom.

While we wait for the ambulance, he whispers something, but I can't make out the words. I lean closer even though he smells really bad. I think he may have pissed himself. He speaks again. It sounds like "Kill me." Or maybe "You killed me." It's either a command or an accusation. I feel as if I've stuck my finger in a light socket—buzzed and disoriented and paralyzed. Have I killed him? Would I? Should I? If someone wants to die, which is worse—the accidental or the intentional? How can I even ask that question? My stomach heaves, and I have to swallow hard to keep from puking.

When the ambulance finally arrives, the paramedics confirm that he's had a full-blown stroke.

"Good thing you were here," one of them says. Oh yeah, right, I think. I almost blurt out something about not calling soon enough, but instead I just watch dumbly as they bundle Arthur up and lift him into the ambulance. I climb in and sit next to him. As we drive away from the house, sirens blaring and lights flashing, he speaks again, two words, his voice almost a gargle. This time I know what he's saying: "Kill me."

Twelve

Time both slows down and speeds up after Arthur goes into the hospital. When I'm away from him, the summer seems to be zooming by in a blur of bike rides, trips to the gym and hanging out with Dani. When I'm with him, time creeps along like a slug on a damp dark trail.

Being with Arthur is more painful than any bed of nails, but I need to do penance, to atone. For not calling 9-1-1 sooner. For calling 9-1-1 when I did. For wishing him dead. For trying to keep him alive. It's my hair shirt, my whip, my karma. And yeah, I know I'm getting my dogmas mixed up. I've drawn the line at two of the most common forms of penance though: fasting and celibacy. I can't fast because I figure I need my strength to bike the ten miles out to the hospital a few times a week, and I can't take a vow of celibacy in case, well, in case I have a chance with Dani. She thinks it's sweet that I care so much about my grandfather. She'd probably hate me if she knew the truth.

When Arthur was first admitted, he was in acute care; now he's in the geriatric rehab ward. In the days right after the stroke, Mom had almost hourly consultations with the doctors and nurses, who told her that I saved Arthur's life by calling 9-1-1 right away. I know better. So does Arthur. I'm waiting for him to tell the world what a selfish little shit I am, how I stood beside him with my phone in my hand and had a philosophical debate with myself before calling for help. Although how he would know that is beyond me. Some kind of old-person superpower, maybe.

One day, while I'm sitting in Arthur's room watching him sleep, I start thinking—worrying, really—about what to do next. Maybe it's not too late to take off in the T-bird. Arthur won't care, and if I'm going to go, I need to go soon. School's about to start. If I stay here, I'll have to make new friends, buy new clothes, maybe grow my hair a bit. If I go back to Nova Scotia, I'll have to find a crappy place to stay and work at a shitty job after school and on weekends. I probably won't even have time to hang out with my friends. Peaches will find another guy. Hell, she probably already has. It won't be the same.

Suddenly Arthur speaks. "I never went to university, you know." It's like he's reading my mind, which is pretty freaky. He struggles to sit up and swats me away when I try to help him get all his pillows into place. It's painful to watch him drag his withered body into a sitting position, but I understand why he wants to do it himself. I remember feeling that way when I was a little kid and Mom was always trying to help me. Tying your own shoelaces, sitting up in bed—it's not so different. It's all about independence. Or the illusion of independence anyway.

I sit down and wait for him to speak again. When he doesn't, I nudge his foot and say, "How come?"

"How come what?"

"How come you never went to university?"

"No time," he grunts. "Everyone said I should concentrate on my music. But they were wrong."

"Yeah? You did all right."

"It was only one thing. And when it was gone—there was nothing left." He holds up his twisted hands. "Less than nothing."

"How would going to university have changed that?" I ask. "What would you have studied?"

His answer takes me by surprise. I would have guessed English or philosophy, but he says, "Physics." It's so out in left field that I laugh.

"Physics? You would have studied physics? Why?"

He glares at me and says, "It doesn't matter now. I educated myself but it wasn't the same. I memorized poetry, read all the classics, taught myself French and Italian, read every book about physics I could get my hands on, but I didn't have anyone to talk to about it. All anyone ever wanted from me was my music, so I gave them that. I thought it was the right thing to do."

"It can't have been so wrong," I say. "You're famous." And rich, but I don't say that out loud.

"It wasn't enough. Don't make the same mistake."

"Okay," I say. "I'll go to university. I promise." I was planning to anyway, so I'm not even lying.

"What will you study?" he asks. He's never taken this much interest in anything about me, except maybe my sex life, or lack of it, so I think about it a bit before I answer.

"Math." The minute I say it, I know it's true. I love math. Always have. It makes sense to me.

"Math, eh? Music's all about math, did you know that?"

I shake my head.

"There's a book," he says. "*Emblems of Mind*. You should read it."

"Okay," I say again. His eyes are closing and he's slipping sideways on his pillows. I help him lie down. This time he doesn't push me away.

.

"When's Arthur coming home?" I ask Mom as we drive to the hospital for what seems like the thousandth time. It's been almost three weeks since his stroke, and I've logged a lot of hours at the hospital. I no longer wake up every day and think, Today's the day I take the T-bird and head East. I'm not sure exactly when it happened, but I've started thinking of Victoria as home.

"Home?" Mom sighs. "I have no idea. Maybe never."

"Never?" It hasn't really occurred to me that Arthur won't get better, that he won't sit in front of his TV and yell at the news anchors on CNN. That he won't yell at me.

"He needs so much care," Mom says. "He won't be able to manage on his own."

"So what will happen to him?"

"I'm looking at long-term care facilities."

"Nursing homes, you mean."

"They don't call them that anymore."

"But that's what they are."

"Some of them are very good. Quite homey. Lots of opportunities for socializing."

"Arthur will hate that," I say.

"I know, Rolly," Mom says. "Believe me, I know."

We ride the rest of the way in silence, and when we get to the hospital, Mom goes off to have a meeting with Arthur's team, which consists of a geriatrician, a dietitian, a physiotherapist, an occupational therapist, a speech therapist and a social worker. According to Arthur, they are all, with the exception of the speech therapist, incompetent cretins. According to Mom, they are patient, hard-working health care professionals who only have Arthur's best interests at heart. From my limited observation, they're somewhere in between, depending on the day and Arthur's mood. Arthur is right though. The exception is Lars, the speech therapist, who looks like a middle-aged Norse god—handsome but a bit beat-up, what with all that cold weather and warfare and human sacrifice. Mom says he looks like Nick Nolte circa 1990, "when he was hot." Which must mean she thinks Lars is hot, which is weird and maybe, I don't know, vaguely unethical. He is part of Arthur's "team," after all. Lars doesn't take any shit from anyone, Arthur included. If you want to learn to talk again, Lars is your guy. If you don't, well, step aside.

Arthur bonded with Lars immediately and his speech is improving rapidly. The slur has almost disappeared, and he doesn't have nearly as much trouble finding the right words for things. He's forgotten some stuff, like my nickname (which is good) and his kids' names (which is bad), but Mom takes it all in stride. Aunt Marta doesn't. She told Mom a while ago that she won't come to visit until Arthur remembers her name. Mom called her a word I've never heard her use before, and they haven't talked since.

I stop at the hospital coffee shop to pick up a coffee and a chocolate-glazed donut for Arthur. That's our ritual: I bring coffee so Arthur can complain that it's not a *café au lait*. Once in a while I go to Starbucks and get him a latte, but he still bitches at me.

Today when I get there, he's waiting for me by the elevator in his wheelchair.

"What took you so long?" he growls.

"Good to see you too," I reply. "Where do you want to go? Your room? The lounge?"

"Home."

I don't know what to say. I have no idea when he's getting out, but I'm pretty sure he won't be going home. He's like a baby that's learning to walk: he can only go about ten steps before he starts to topple over. "I brought you a donut and coffee. Let's go to the lounge. Maybe watch some TV." I start to wheel him away from the elevator, hoping that he'll be distracted by the possibility of a *Little House* rerun.

"I want to sleep in my own bed," he says. "The noise here is unbearable. The lights are always on. Someone's always poking at me or asking me questions."

"At least you've got a private room now," I remind him. "Remember that dude you shared with when you first came? What was his name?"

"Chuck," Arthur says. "His name was Chuck Callahan and he had never heard of Mozart. And he snored like a chain saw going through a sequoia."

Why does he remember Chuck's name, but not my mom's? It doesn't seem fair. And where does a word like *sequoia* come from when he often can't remember simple words like *milk* or *book*. I know it's something to do with how the stroke damaged his brain, but it still freaks me out. I mean, we're all walking around with this amazing, delicate spongy *thing* inside our skulls, and we totally take for granted that the wires won't get crossed—until they do, and it's too late.

"His family brought food in buckets," Arthur continues. "Chicken. What kind of people eat food out of buckets? Like pigs at a trough. The smell was disgusting."

"That's why they call it pigging out. You oughtta try it sometime," I say. "It's good. I'll bring you some. Fatten you up."

We turn into the lounge, where two old ladies are playing a card game, and an old man has fallen asleep on the flowered couch. The TV is on, but it's muted. Oprah's audience is crying again. One of the old ladies looks up and smiles at Arthur.

She has bright blue eyes, and she's wearing hot pink lipstick with fingernails to match. A multicolored scarf is tied in her white curls. From the neck down, she is standard-issue geriatric-ward patient, female variety: fluffy pink robe, slippers to match, walker at her side.

"Ah, the famous Mr. Jenkins," she says. "Care to join us?" She waves her hand at the cards. "We can always accommodate an extra player, can't we, Leah?"

The other old lady (pale blue robe, green slippers, red lipstick on her teeth) smiles and nods.

"How about it, Arthur?" I say.

He shakes his head and covers his eyes with one hand, as if that will make him invisible.

"Take me home, Royce," he quavers. "I want to go home."

The old ladies look at each other and make soft clucking noises, like giant pastel chickens confronted with an ailing rooster.

"Sorry, ladies. Guess he's not up for it today." I turn the wheelchair around and start down the corridor to Arthur's room. He keeps his head down and his face hidden until we get to his room and I help him into bed. I wipe the tears from his face and get him to blow his nose before I hand him his donut and coffee.

"You okay?" I ask. I'm not sure why he was crying— the thought of playing cards with old ladies, maybe— but I've been told that mood swings and paranoia are common with stroke patients.

I'm not too surprised when he says, "They're after me, you know."

"Who?"

"The merry widows. I'm rich and famous. They think I'm a good catch."

"Jeez, Arthur, they just wanted to play cards, not marry you."

"Don't be stupid," he replies. "You can see it in their eyes. The greed."

"No way, Arthur. They were just being friendly."

"Don't argue with me, boy. This coffee's cold. Get me another."

A couple of times a week I ride over to Arthur's house to take in the mail and start the car. I resist the temptation to take it out for a spin, although I wonder what Dani would think if I pulled up outside her house in a '56 T-Bird. Maybe some day, when I have my proper license, we'll go on a real date: dinner, movie, sex in the backseat of the car. Very 1950s.

My paycheck ended when Arthur went into the hospital, but Mom hasn't said anything to me about getting another job. Since I'm no longer saving for a car, I spend money on haircuts, bike gear, clothes and a membership at the Y. My stash is dwindling fast. Too fast. I wonder if one of the bike shops in town might hire me. I don't think much about Lunenburg anymore. Peaches' status on Facebook is "dating." There are tons of pictures of her with my buddy, Lewis. I don't have any right to be upset. But it still hurts. If Dani and I were a couple, which we're not, I could post some pictures of my own. Instead I ride out to the hospital after lunch on Monday, Wednesday and Friday. Arthur has to do rehab stuff every morning—he hates it, but it's not optional—so on the afternoons I visit, he bitches about it to me. Mom still does the weekend shifts.

By the middle of August he's doing a lot better, and sometimes I forget to feel guilty that he's ended up here.

In many ways, he's back to being the old Arthur: irascible, rude and crude. His gait (as his physio calls it) is almost back to normal and he wants to go home. He still doesn't know that he can't. Mom has finally found a suitable nursing home for him and put him on the waiting list. I refuse to call it a "care facility," which pisses Mom off, but she's too busy "liaising" with all the various caregivers and institutions to give me a hard time. I notice that she "liaises" quite a lot with Lars, if you can call going out for dinner "liaising." Lars comes to pick her up in a truck identical to hers, but dirtier, which makes them both laugh way too much. In the back of Lars's truck is a dirt bike, strapped down, and a gigantic dog, not strapped down. The dog, which turns out to be a Great Dane (ha ha) named Beowulf, is, thank god, well-trained. I'm not crazy about big dogs. I still have the scars on my arm from when a German shepherd took what its owner called a "playful nip" at me in a playground. I was three at the time. My mom took a "playful nip" at the woman's head with her backpack.

When Lars calls the dog, it leaps over the tailgate and lopes over to where Lars is standing with his arm around my mom, who is grinning and tucking her hair behind her ears, a sure sign she is nervous. Lars is like an unexpected windfall—both welcome and disconcerting.

"Sit, Beowulf," he says.

Beowulf sits. Even sitting, he is huge. Mom giggles nervously and says, "He's as big as a small pony."

"But cuter," says the Norse God. "Like you."

Is he saying my mom is cuter than a small pony? That seems a bit odd, but Mom giggles again and pets Beowulf's massive head, at which point I hop on my bike and leave them to their animal husbandry, or whatever.

Two months of biking everywhere has changed me. So have regular visits to the weight room at the Y. My thighs ripple inside my bike shorts, my calves bulge above my cleated bike shoes. My chest fills out my expensive skin-tight V-neck moisture-wicking shirt, my biceps are modestly magnificent. I can ride out to the hospital without breaking a sweat. I can sit on the beach with Dani without fear of mockery. I have a six pack. So does Dani, whose idea of a good time is a push-up competition. All I can do is try to keep up.

The day I introduce Dani to Arthur, we ride out to her favorite lake first. It's a long way, but it's worth it. In the middle of the week, there aren't many people—just a few families with little kids who stay close to shore— and we lock our bikes up and race to the water, shedding our clothes as we run. We swim to the center of the lake, where we lie on our backs and flutter our arms and legs just enough to stay afloat. Once in a while we stop fluttering and let ourselves sink for a moment. When I come to the surface and open my eyes, I see an eagle swoop down into the top of a cedar. We drift away from the beach, fluttering, sinking, fluttering, sinking, sinking.

I feel something brush my foot, my leg, my chest. Weeds? Not this far from shore. A fish? Not likely. I kick to the surface, and Dani pops up beside me, spouting like a whale. She tips her head back and laughs. Was it her hand that ran the length of my body? Even in the cold water, the thought of it makes my dick stiffen. I really like her, but I'm waiting for her to make the first move. Was that it?

"Race you to the shore," she yells.

She beats me, but it's close. My hard-on has disappeared by the time I get to shore, but makes a reappearance as she towels off in front of me. I turn away and struggle into my shirt and shoes, visualizing Arthur's gnarled toenails, his copious ear hair, his bedside commode. My erection subsides. I can almost hear Arthur's voice. "Don't say I never did anything for you, boy."

When I turn around, Dani is dressed and ready to go, her hair braided into a long wet rope down her back.

"You sure you're ready for this?" I ask. "This" being Arthur.

"Sure," Dani replies. "I want to meet him. My parents can't stop talking about how great he is, and you can't stop talking about what a pain he is. I need to find out which is true."

"Both."

"Both?"

"Yeah. You'll see."

She hops on her bike, and I follow her, admiring her ass and almost wiping out on a pothole in the process. When we get to the hospital, we're all sweaty again and out of breath. When we get to Arthur's room, the first thing out of his mouth is, "Glad to see you're finally getting some, boy."

Thirteen

There's a moment of silence after Arthur speaks. Then Dani strides over to his wheelchair, crouches down beside him, puts her face about an inch from his and says, "I've heard a lot about you, Mr. Jenkins, but I've never heard you were rude or crude, so just this once I'm going to give you a do-over."

"A what?" Arthur barks.

"A do-over. A re-wind. A chance for you to get it right." She gets up, grabs my hand and drags me out of the room. Arthur doesn't say a word, but I turn and catch a glimpse of his face as I go. His face is scarlet. The great Arthur Jenkins is blushing.

"That was...amazing," I say as Dani plops herself down on the ugly orange couch by the elevator. "Awesome."

She punches me—hard—on the shoulder.

"What was that for?"

"For not doing it yourself."

"Not doing what myself? Calling him on his shit?"

She nods and turns away from me to stare out the window at some bunnies that are nibbling the shrubs in the hospital's tiny garden. I'm still trying to process what she said and whether it means that she likes me. Or not.

"I-I'm sorry," I stutter. "It's complicated—"

"Complicated how?"

For a second I toy with the idea of telling her that it's my fault Arthur is here, but I want her to like me.

"Family shit," I mumble. "You know. Relationships. Like I said, it's complicated."

She stares at the bunnies some more and then turns to me and smiles. Her teeth are white, but a bit crooked, as if she'd taken off her braces too soon.

"It's okay, Royce. I get it. It's not like you didn't warn me." She stands up and we walk back to Arthur's room. He's sitting by his window, watching the bunnies destroy an azalea. He turns when he hears us walk in and heaves himself to his feet as we approach. I can see by the tiny beads of sweat on his forehead that it is taking all his strength to stand. I put my hand on his elbow to steady him as he holds out his hand to Dani, who takes it and leans forward to kiss his whiskery cheek.

"Arthur, this is Dani. Dani, this is Arthur." He's starting to wobble, so I ease him back into the wheelchair. Dani pulls up the visitor's chair beside him.

"It's an honor to meet you, sir," she says. "My parents are big fans."

"The honor is all mine, my dear," he says. "Please forgive an old man's rudeness."

"No worries," she says. "Do you want to go visit the bunnies? Maybe have a picnic?" We all look down at the little garden, which has a few bistro tables and chairs under big green umbrellas.

Arthur nods, and I head to the coffee shop to get some food while Dani wheels him out to the garden. When I join them, Arthur is sitting in the sun with his eyes closed. A tiny smile plays around his cracked lips.

"Reminds me of Paris," he says. "The Tuileries."

"You sat with a cute chick in the Tuileries?" I say. "Nice."

Dani laughs and hands Arthur a Tim Hortons ham and cheese sandwich and a paper napkin. "Your baguette, *monsieur*."

"*Merci, mademoiselle*," he says, bowing slightly in his wheelchair.

I put his coffee on the bistro table beside him. "*Un café au lait, aussi*."

"*Merci*," he says again. He lifts the paper cup in a shaky toast. "*À votre santé, mes amis*."

"*À votre santé*, Arthur," we reply. To your health.

"Why don't we take the photo albums and the laptop to the hospital," Dani asks one day when we're at Arthur's taking in the mail. I'd shown her the albums one day when we were tired of cards and it was too hot to lie on the deck. We sat side by side on the single bed in the second bedroom, looking at pictures of Arthur in Paris, Arthur in New York, Arthur in London. I wanted to kiss her, but before I got up the nerve, she stood up and went to the kitchen for a soda.

Now she says, "He's not gonna live forever, you know. He needs to tell his story. You need to record it. It's like an oral history. I did one with my great-grandma before she died. And she was a prairie farm wife, not a famous musician. I mean, Arthur's been everywhere. He knew Gloria Vanderbilt, Casals, Picasso even. And he loves talking about himself—you told me that."

"Okay, okay," I say. "I get it. He's an interesting dude. Did I tell you he knows Bono?" I throw it out there like it's nothing—a cotton ball of a fact— but I know it will impress her. She thinks Bono is awesome. Right up there with Barack Obama and Jane Goodall.

Dani's eyes open wide. "You're shittin' me. He knows Bono? Arthur's more than interesting, Rolly. He's"—she searches for the right word—"significant."

Dani found out my nickname from Mom, who let it slip one day when we were hanging out at my place. Dani thinks it's "adorable," so I let her use it when we're alone. Not in public though. Never in public. And never around Arthur.

The next day we pack the albums in cardboard boxes that I get from the grocery store, and I make sure I've got the cord for the laptop. Mom drives us out to the hospital, where she's having a "meeting" with Lars before she goes to work.

"Good luck with the Arthurian legend," Mom says as she heads off to find Lars.

"Thanks for the ride, Ms. Peterson," Dani says. "Great title, huh, Rolly? *The Arthurian Legend.*"

I grunt as I lift out the last of the boxes. I have no idea where I'm going to put six cardboard boxes in Arthur's room. I'm still not convinced this is a good idea, but as Dani points out, it beats listening to Arthur complain about the hospital food, the other patients, the staff, the room, his family and the fact that he gets no respect.

Dani is right: Arthur practically drools at the prospect of talking about himself for hours on end. "*The Arthurian Legend,*" he repeats. "I like that. When do we start?"

"Right now, if you like," Dani says, pulling the first album out of a box. "You ready, Royce?"

I nod. The laptop is set up on one of those adjustable bed tables, and I'm propped up on Arthur's bed with about five pillows at my back. I figure I might as well be comfortable. Dani pulls a chair close to Arthur's, opens the album and asks a couple of questions. I type as Arthur speaks. Dani asks the odd question, nudging Arthur for details or moving him along. Once in a while, I ask him to slow down, but mostly I can keep up. When Arthur identifies a person or a place in a photograph, Dani writes down the info on a sticky note and puts it next to the picture.

After an hour, Arthur is tired and my fingers are cramping. Dani closes the album and pats Arthur on the check. I close the laptop and shove the table to one side.

"See you tomorrow," we say.

"*À bientôt*," Arthur replies.

After that, Arthur and I really get into a groove. Whenever I visit, I bring him coffee and set up the laptop. Then I type while he sips his coffee and talks. I don't want to be impressed, but I can't help it. Not just by all the celebrities he knew (Jackie Kennedy Onassis, Bill Clinton, Frank Sinatra, Muhammed Ali—the list goes on and on), but by his accomplishments: the symphonies he played with, the platinum albums, the sold-out concerts at Carnegie Hall.

What really interests me, though, is the family stuff. How he grieved after Marta's mother died. How much he missed Coralee. How much he loves my mother, who never mentioned that he took her to Paris for her sixteenth birthday or that she spent every Christmas and every summer with him until she married my dad.

All she ever told me was that she had round-the-clock nannies until he parked her at a boarding school when she was five. No mention of summers in the house in Provence or skiing in Gstaad with the British royal family. I didn't even know there *was* a house in Provence let alone a townhouse in New York. I wonder if he still owns them. She can't have forgotten, and he can't be making it all up. The truth—whatever that is—must lie somewhere in between, but the details he provides are crisp and convincing: the color of Princess Diana's eyes, the size of Maria Callas's feet, the taste of *sachertorte* in Vienna. As he gets closer to the present, the fog rolls in and he stumbles over names and dates. He can't remember when he retired to Victoria. He isn't sure where Marta lives. He doesn't know if he's ever been to my house.

Ten days after we start, he pulls the plug on the project. He's in bed when I arrive, so I hand him his coffee, sit down in the visitor's chair, open the laptop and wait for him to speak. Finally he says, "No more."

"No more what?"

He glowers at me. "I can't remember any more."

I look at the laptop screen. "You were telling me about—"

He interrupts. "I'm too tired." He lets his head fall back against the pillow and shuts his eyes. "No more."

I wait, but he is silent. After about ten minutes, he lifts a shaky hand from his lap and points to the door.

"You want me to go?" I ask. I'm offended. No, I'm hurt. I thought we were—I don't know—bonding. I guess I was wrong. I'm just his slave after all. And I'm not even getting paid.

He nods. I move to shut down the laptop, and he says, "No. Leave it alone. Get out."

Asshole, I think as I leave. Now I understand why Mom keeps her distance from him. How many times has she gotten sucked in by his charm, only to be pushed away when he's bored or annoyed or busy? I ride home, raging, calling Arthur every name I can think of: motherfucker, bastard, cocksucker, sonofabitch, ass monkey, dickwad, douchebag. I yell, "Fuck you, you fuckin' fuck," which is lame but surprisingly satisfying, until I realize that the lady in the car beside me at the stop sign looks totally freaked out. I mouth "Sorry," but she just turns away, as if I've let her down. By the time I get home, I feel a bit calmer. I have a long shower, make a turkey sandwich and call Dani. Her voicemail picks up, and I don't leave a message. She'll see that I called. Exhaustion hits me with the force of water from a fire hose, and I collapse onto the couch, asleep the moment my head hits the patchwork pillow.

My cell phone wakes me up. I pick up, expecting to hear Dani's voice, but it's Mom.

"Rolly, he's had another stroke."

I check the time. I've been asleep for four hours.

"When?" I sit up in bed, wide awake. Napping usually makes me groggy, but I feel decidedly alert. Maybe bad news does that—or maybe it's adrenaline.

"A few hours ago. He didn't come down for lunch, so one of the aides went looking for him." Her voice breaks. "This was a big one, Rolly. Worse than the last. They don't know if he'll make it."

As she talks, I get up and head for the bathroom. "I'm on my way, Mom," I say. "I can be there in forty-five minutes."

"You don't need to ride," she says. "Lars is coming for you. Just be ready, okay? And can you bring me a toothbrush and maybe some sweats? I'm going to stay here tonight."

"Sure, Mom," I say.

"You're a good boy," she says.

"See you soon, Mom." I hang up and grab a black garbage bag from the kitchen. By the time Lars arrives, I'm standing outside, ready to go. No dirt bike today, no Beowulf.

I'm grateful he doesn't try to chitchat on the ride to the hospital, apart from saying that he's available to do whatever we need.

All he says is, "Your mom is a great lady. This is very hard for her."

"Don't you think I know that?" I say. He doesn't take it any further. The last thing I want to think about is my mom's love life. I call Dani and leave her a message telling her what's happened and that I'll call her later. I'm kind of glad she doesn't answer. I don't think I can deal with anyone but Mom right now.

Lars drops me off at the front doors, and I run up the stairs to Arthur's room, the garbage bag bumping against my legs. I don't want to be stuck with strangers in the elevator. When I get to his room, Mom is waiting outside in the hallway.

"The nurses are turning him," she says.

"Turning him?"

"He's paralyzed, Rolly." She starts to cry, and I put my arms around her. It's strange, being the one to comfort her.

"But he was paralyzed before," I say into her hair. She shakes her head and mumbles into my shoulder.

"This is much worse. He can't swallow. He can't speak. He doesn't know who I am."

I think about what that means for a minute. He probably won't know me either. "So they'll put him on an IV, right? To feed him."

She nods.

"He's tough, Mom. You always say that."

"I know, Rolly, I know. But this…this is different."

She pulls away from me and wipes her face on her sleeve. "I need to call his lawyer, find out if he had a living will. I should have done it before, but he was doing so well."

"A living will?"

"It's a legal document that says what kind of medical treatment you want if you can't express your wishes verbally. Which he can't. I haven't been able to find one at his house. Can you sit with him while I make a few calls?"

"Sure." The nurse comes out of the room and tells us it's okay to go in.

"He's sleeping," she says. "Poor old fellow. Call me if you need anything."

Mom leaves to make her calls, and I go into the room. Arthur is lying on his back, with the blankets drawn up to his chin. His body looks small, almost childlike, under the covers. His mouth is drawn down on one side in what looks like a snarl. I know it isn't. Tears form in my eyes as I lower myself into the chair by his bed and stroke his arm.

"Hey, Arthur. It's me, Rolly. I'm staying here until Mom comes back. I brought you something."

I pull Mom's portable CD player from the garbage bag and set it up on the night table. I've brought about twenty CDs with me—mostly classical, mostly Arthur. I put one on—Brahms' Double Concerto in A Minor, with Arthur on the cello, Itzhak Perlman on the violin and the Berlin Philharmonic—and sit back as the music fills the room. I've never heard it before, so I read the liner notes and find out that it was Brahms' final work for orchestra and that it was a form of musical reconciliation between Brahms and Joseph Joachim, the violinist he wrote it for. Joachim's motto, which inspired Brahms to write the concerto in F-A-E, was *frei aber einsam*—free but lonely. Sort of says it all. About Arthur anyway. About me too, until a few months ago.

I pull the laptop off the bedside table. Someone has closed it, but it's still plugged in. I open it and the last page of my transcription fills the screen. At the bottom of the page is something I didn't write.

Royce, I know there will be another stroke. I want to die. Please kill me. Arthur.

My hands tremble as I read the words again, remembering what he said after the first stroke: *Kill me.* I was kidding myself, thinking it might have been an accusation. Now that I have it in black and white, there's no room for discussion, no ambiguity. He wants me to end it. Snuff him out. Turn out the lights. I delete the words on the screen and click on *Empty Trash.* The words disappear, but they are etched in my brain. *Please kill me.* At least he asked nicely.

I'm totally confused. And angry. I didn't sign on for this. How can he be so selfish? What he's asking me to do is every kind of wrong. Isn't it? I'm only sixteen, for god's sake. My life would be over too if I got caught snuffing him out. But what kind of life is he going to have now? I look at him—paralyzed, mute, catheterized—and I know the answer: no life at all. Maybe he doesn't mean that he wants me, personally, to kill him. Maybe this is just his version of a living will. Maybe I shouldn't have erased it.

The rage subsides and is replaced by a tsunami of sadness. I look at the shriveled figure on the bed and it hits me: Arthur—grumpy, brilliant, infuriating, smelly Arthur—is never coming back. He needs me to do one last thing for him. I can almost hear him say, "Just do it, you pussy," like a demented Nike ad. I take a deep breath. The music flows over me as I pick up a pillow and place it over his face. I hold it there—one second, two, three, four, five. My hands start to shake and when a muffled moan leaks through the pillow, I jump back and fling the pillow across the room.

When Mom comes into the room, she finds me sitting by the window, head back and eyes closed. I have spent the last ten minutes breathing deeply and evenly, trying to calm my racing heart. I have managed to stop crying, but I can't believe she won't notice something different about me. I have, after all, just tried to murder her father. Surely it shows.

I lift my head and slowly open my eyes.

"Did you talk to the lawyer?" I ask.

She nods and sighs. I can tell by the look on her face that it hasn't gone well.

"No living will," I state. Except the one I erased.

She shakes her head. "His lawyer tried to get him to do one a while ago, but he refused. Said he trusted me to do the right thing when the time came. We'll have to decide what to do. You and me and Marta. When the time comes."

I nod. I can't speak. I know I should say, "He wants to die, Mom," but I can't. There's no proof anymore. I just deleted it. Put it in the tiny trash can because it freaked me out. I tried to do what he wanted. I failed. I don't want Mom to think badly of him. Or me. I thought he had the right to die. And I still couldn't pull the trigger. Did that make me a coward or a saint?

"We don't have to decide anything today," she adds.

"Okay," I say.

The final notes of the Brahms die away. A tiny sigh comes from the form on the bed.

Fourteen

Arthur improves, but at a glacial rate. Mom has to take him off the list for the nursing home she found because he needs way more care than they can provide. I go with her when she visits other potential facilities. Some places are downright disgusting—you wouldn't send a dog you hated there—some are like prisons, with locked wards for the Alzheimer patients. Some have lobbies like luxury hotels, but the residents' wards are pretty much the same everywhere. Carpeted or not, potpourri notwithstanding, ugly art aside, the smell is overpowering—part industrial-strength cleanser, part bodily fluids, part overcooked vegetables. In some places the inmates are dressed and tooling around with expensive walkers, playing bridge, singing "Wait 'Till the

Sun Shines Nellie," doing chair yoga. In other places, the corridors are lined with people slumped in wheelchairs, staring into space, catheter bags filling up, stained hospital gowns gaping to reveal veined legs and swollen ankles. There are far more women than men. At one place, the director of care, a woman in a designer suit, refers to the facility as "the Cadillac of care facilities." For some reason, this strikes Mom and me as hysterically funny and we both burst out laughing. The woman frowns as Mom stands and picks up her purse.

"I'm sorry," Mom says between snorts. "A Cadillac? That just wouldn't suit my father. Maybe a BMW or a Mercedes, but a Cadillac? I think not. So *nouveau riche*." This sends us both into another fit of giggles. We shake hands with the bewildered director and run out to the truck, where I pound the dashboard and Mom bangs her head on the steering wheel. I haven't laughed so hard since my friend Doug shot Coke out his nose at my tenth birthday party.

Eventually we find a place that will take Arthur as soon as they have room. Translation: as soon as one of the residents dies. In the meantime, Arthur continues his daily routine: speech therapy, occupational therapy, physiotherapy, meds, diaper changes, sponge baths, iv feeding. When I visit, he's often asleep. If he's awake, he looks right through me, even when I talk to him. Mom thinks there was a moment when he tried to say

her name, but even with Lars's help, his speech is inde-
cipherable. When he does try to speak, he usually gets
so frustrated that he gives up and sulks. Every time
I see him, I relive those few seconds when I held the
pillow over his face. If I'd had the guts, he wouldn't be
suffering. Sorry, Arthur, you picked the wrong guy.

School is starting soon, and I won't be able to visit
very often. Dani is excited about going back to school;
me, not so much. I still don't know very many people.
She's introduced me to a few of her friends. The guys
seem pretty cool; they even invited me to go off-road
biking with them and offered to lend me a mountain
bike. It's all so…normal.

I feel like a fraud hanging out with them.

I don't see Dani as much as I would like, although
she seems okay with it. She's not clingy, that's for sure.
She's warned me that she gets pretty busy in the fall—
not a promising sign—but she hasn't shut me down
either. Glass half full, right? Sometimes she comes out to
the hospital with me to visit Arthur, whom she entertains
with anecdotes about her catering job, her little sister
Lisa, her dog Yoda. Once in a while, the non-paralyzed
side of his face creases into what might be a smile, but for
the most part he looks like he's made of granite. Granite
that can cry. The nurses tell me he's not really crying,
it's just that when his eyes water, he can't blink the tears
away. He looks pretty sad to me.

I keep playing music for him, since I run out of things to say pretty quickly. My stories seem boring compared to Dani's: I don't have a little sister or a dog or even an amusing goldfish. So I alternate between my CDs, my mom's and his: The Killers, Yehudi Menuhin, Metallica, Glenn Gould, James Taylor. I even find an old three-CD set called *The Best from Broadway Musicals*. The first CD, which is all Andrew Lloyd Webber, stays in the case. That's one thing Arthur and I agree on: Andrew Lloyd Webber is the anti-Christ. *The Phantom of the Opera* sucks ass. The second CD is all Rodgers and Hammerstein songs, the third is Irving Berlin. When I was little, Mom used to play me to sleep with show tunes, so I know all the words to "Oh, What a Beautiful Morning" and "Shall We Dance." It's not something I usually tell people. I'm less familiar with the Berlin songs, but I can still hum along and, it turns out, so can Arthur. At first I think there's something wrong with the CD, but then I realize that the strange scratchy noise is coming from the bed. Arthur is humming along to "Anything You Can Do (I Can Do Better)" from *Annie Get Your Gun*. He's not getting every note, and he sounds like he has a mouthful of mashed potatoes, but his pitch isn't half bad. When the song comes to an end, I push the Pause button and give him a standing ovation.

"Nice work, Arthur," I say. "Good song choice. Could be your theme song."

Of course he doesn't reply. I press *Play*, and he hums along to "Hello, Young Lovers." I rummage through the bag of CDs and find an old CD of my mom's, a greatest hits package from the thirties and forties: "Inka-Dinka-Doo," "My Heart Belongs to Daddy," "Indian Love Call." He knows them all. I switch to Mozart, and the humming stops. Back to Ella Fitzgerald crooning, "Lover Come Back to Me," and he's at it again. Chopin is greeted with silence. I only stop when the nurse comes in to check his diaper and to see if he has bed sores. They always ask me to leave, which is fine by me.

I run into Lars on my way out. When I ask him how he thinks Arthur is, he replies very slowly and deliberately, as if he has trouble forming words. I wonder if he has had speech therapy himself for some long-ago injury. Then I remember Mom saying that English is Lars's second language. He also speaks German and French, apparently. So European.

"I think he is getting better," Lars says. "But you have to be patient. It is a long process."

"Did you know he can hum?" I ask.

"Hum?" Lars sounds as if he doesn't know what humming is.

"Yeah, you know." I hum a bit of "Happy Birthday." "He hums."

"When?"

"Like, just now."

"You're sure?"

"Yeah, I'm sure. I've been playing music for him every day. When he hears show tunes, he hums along. He's got perfect pitch."

"This is amazing."

"It is?"

"Yes. I thought it was too soon."

"Too soon?"

"For MIT. Melodic Intonation Therapy. It is a way of helping stroke patients with speech recovery. I just took a workshop. I was hoping to use some of the techniques with Arthur, but you are way ahead of me." The more excited Lars gets, the stronger his accent gets and the faster he talks. I wonder if he reverts to Danish when he's really juiced. Like when he has sex. I yank my mind like it's a dog on a choke chain and get it back on track.

"So it's a good thing?" I ask.

"Definitely. Simply put, it means his right brain is assisting his damaged left brain."

"But it's just humming, not words."

"It is not *just* humming; it is evidence. Evidence that things are going on in his brain. Positive things. Words may be next. Listen closely." Lars's beeper goes off, and he glances down at it and says something rude to it in Danish. At least it sounds like Danish and it sounds rude. It could be Norwegian, for all I know.

"I have to go," he says. "We will talk again, yah?"

"I guess. But what should I do?" I ask as he jogs off down the hall.

"Keep playing the music."

"That's it?"

"For now," he calls over his shoulder.

I go back to school after Labor Day, and it's surprisingly okay. My teachers seem nice enough, and a couple of Dani's guy friends are in my classes. She's got a lot of guy friends. We hardly ever see each other at school, except in math class and wood shop. Yeah, Dani's taking shop, which lots of girls do, just like lots of guys take cooking. And yes, she's better at it than me. I make my mom a spice rack; Dani makes an inlaid coffee table. She's been taking shop for a few years, and her dad is a cabinetmaker, so I don't feel too bad. She's looks pretty cute in her goggles, handling the band saw like a pro. But I'm better at math, so we help each other out. On the weekends she has music lessons and dance classes and all kinds of rehearsals, so there's not much time for a relationship, even if she wanted one, which she doesn't seem to.

I don't see Arthur as often as I did before school started, and I feel guilty about that. Guilt is my new go-to emotion. When I do go, he's often asleep, and if he's awake, he can't speak. He's still on the IV, but he's wasting away: he looks like a concentration camp survivor. His eyes follow me as I move around the room, and all I see in them is accusation. I fail him every time

I visit. I know that. But I can't do what he asked me to do. Not now. Not after the humming. So I sit with him and listen to music and look at his photo albums while he hums and glares.

In my favorite picture, which is in the album marked 1937–40, he's sitting astride his fire-engine-red Indian Chief motorcycle, wearing gauntlet-style gloves, knee-high black boots, and a brown leather bomber jacket. Around his neck is a white scarf. A pair of goggles is pushed up onto his head. He is smiling—no, he is laughing—his head tipped slightly back, his mouth open. Whoever took the picture must have been laughing too, since the picture is slightly out of focus. I look over at the figure on the bed and then back at the man in the picture. How does this happen? Where has the laughing Arthur gone? Is he locked away inside the frail, twisted body, or has he long since shriveled up and blown away like a leaf in winter? If he's still in there, will he ever reappear? If he's not there, why are we keeping him alive? Is there any way of knowing? The doctors and nurses and therapists write up reports and discuss his care with Mom, who takes even the smallest bit of progress as a sign that he might yet come back to us. We never discuss whether we're doing the right thing. In the absence of a living will, Mom (and Marta, I suppose) have adopted a "one day at a time" approach, which avoids the whole issue. In other words, they are doing nothing. I, too, have decided to do nothing, but for different reasons. Simply put, as Lars would say, I am a coward.

I close the album and put it back in the box. Louis Armstrong is singing, or rather growling, that it's a wonderful world, which strikes me as kind of funny in a morbid sort of way, given the circumstances. Arthur is humming, and then suddenly he is singing. Three words. *"Skies of blue."* I'm sure of it.

I get up and sit next to him so I can hear him better. His breath reeks, and they haven't shaved him today. I should bring in his electric razor or call Kim and get her to come by and tidy him up. The thought of Kim in this sterile room is disconcerting; it would be like seeing an orchid growing out of a snowbank. Arthur opens his eyes and hums some more. I wait for him to sing another word—*tree of greens* or *red roses too* or *clouds of white*. I even sing along to encourage him. His bad hand, the paralyzed one, twitches, grazing my thigh. I jump up as if he's pinched me. I feel like I've witnessed a miracle, like the face of Jesus in a bowl of Cheerios. I should run and tell somebody, but I don't want the room to fill up with people. I don't want to have to move aside so that Arthur can be poked and prodded. I just want to sit here and listen to him hum.

When he finally drifts off to sleep, without singing or saying another word, I go in search of Lars, but he's left for the day. I call Dani, even though I know she's at a band practice. I get her voicemail, but I don't leave a message. I call my mom, but she's out, probably with Lars. I ride home, do my homework, watch some TV and go to bed. The next morning when I get up, there is a note from Mom on the kitchen table.

Arthur had another stroke in the night. Lars is taking me to the hospital. Go to school. Keep your cell phone on. Don't worry. XO Mom.

My first thought is: Was Lars here overnight?

Fifteen

I don't go to school, and I don't answer the phone until Mom calls, even though Dani texts throughout the morning: *Where r u? Is something wrong?* I try to force myself out of bed and onto my bike, but I'm not sure if I want to ride to school or to the hospital, so I stay where I am. I can't face Dani's concern any more than I can face what's happened to Arthur. Mom calls around noon.

"He's stabilized, Rolly."

"What does that mean, exactly?"

She hesitates. "It means...he's out of immediate danger, I guess."

Immediate danger. Like an avalanche or a charging grizzly.

"Did they shave him yet?" I ask. "Brush his teeth?"

"What?"

"He looked like crap yesterday, Mom. Like no one cared."

Mom starts to cry, and I realize she thinks I mean she doesn't care.

"I didn't mean you, Mom. I meant the people at the hospital. Isn't that what they're paid for?"

She gives a strangled laugh. I wonder if I should tell her that Arthur spoke—that he sang—yesterday. Would it make things worse or better? I can't decide, so I keep my mouth shut. The secrets I'm swallowing make me feel bloated and lethargic, as if I've suddenly gained fifty pounds.

Mom tells me it's okay if I don't come out—Arthur is sleeping and heavily medicated. Lars is going to take her out for lunch and then she'll come home and have a shower and a nap before he takes her back to the hospital. He doesn't think she should be driving.

"I'll be there soon," I tell her. No way do I want to be here when Lars brings her home. For all I know she's planning to shower and nap with him. I just can't deal with that right now. I know I should be happy for her, I know Lars is helping her through a bad time, but it still seems disloyal to Arthur. To me. Maybe I should have taken the T-Bird and made a run for it when I could. Everyone would have been happier.

I'm at the hospital within the hour. Arthur's room is empty, the bed flat and smooth, the IV pole gone. A prickly sweat floods my body, and I feel as if I'm going to pass out. I sit down on the end of the bed, put my head between my legs and wait for the wave of terror to fade. Questions fizz through my brain. Is Arthur dead? Where is his body? Does Mom know? Why didn't she wake me up last night? Why did I lie in bed all morning? Why isn't Mom here? Where is all Arthur's stuff? I jump up and run to the nurses' station, yelling, "Where is Arthur Jenkins?" at an RN I've never seen before. Her name tag says *Marnie*. She seems to be moving in slo-mo as she pulls out a chart and reads it, her lips moving as she runs a finger down the page. When she looks up she says, "And you are?"

I want to punch her and grab the chart from her pudgy hands, but I grit my teeth and say, "His grandson."

"His grandson. Oh yeah, Royce. I heard about you. Your granddad was moved to Intensive Care last night. One floor up."

I'm already on my way to the elevator when I hear her say, "I'm sorry, dear."

Why is she sorry? I find out when I get to the ICU. A nurse stops me at the door and asks me who I'm visiting. When I tell her, she takes me into a small office and sits me down, which is almost as frightening as not finding Arthur in his room.

"Are you close to your grandfather, Royce?"

Am I? I think about her question for a minute and then I nod.

"When was the last time you saw him, Royce?"

"Yesterday afternoon. He was…okay. I mean, he was…the same." I don't tell her about the singing or the way his hand touched my leg. It's private, between him and me. Not her business.

"I need to prepare you a bit before you see him, Royce." I wish she'd stop using my name. It's like she's had lessons on how to speak with distraught family members, which come to think of it, she probably has. Always use their names. Make eye contact. As if on cue, she looks me in the eye and says, "It can be very upsetting. He has a tube in his nose that goes into his stomach, for feeding. There's also a tube in his mouth—it's called an endotracheal tube—that's attached to a mechanical ventilator. There are a lot of wires attached to monitors. We need to keep an eye on his various…functions. He's catheterized, and of course there's an iv for medications. It can be a shock to see someone you love like that." She stops to see how I am taking it.

"So he's basically on life support?"

She hesitates before she answers, as if she wishes someone else were there to give me the answer. "Yes."

"Can I see him now?"

She gets up and says, "You have to wash first and put on a mask and gown. We've had another superbug outbreak. You can stay for fifteen minutes. No more."

"Okay." She shows me where to scrub up, and where to find the gowns, which are made of a ludicrously cheerful Hawaiian print. Palm trees and hula girls.

An alternate universe. When I'm ready, she leads me to one of the glass-walled cubicles that surround the nurses' station like cells in a honeycomb. The only noise in the room is the rhythmic *swish* of the ventilator. Arthur looks even smaller than he did yesterday, as if each successive stroke is shrinking him. Even though I have been prepared, I am not prepared. No one ever could be. The body on the bed is not Arthur. I am as sure of that as I am of my own name, but I know I need to say something.

"Hey, Arthur," I say. "It's me—Rolly."

I sit on the edge of his bed while the nurse checks his vital signs.

"Can he hear me?" I ask.

"Your guess is as good as mine," she replies. "It can't hurt to talk to him, and it might help. Lots of people think it does."

"Can I bring in a CD player? He loves music."

"Maybe tomorrow," she says as she leaves the room. "Fifteen minutes, Royce."

I nod. As soon as she leaves the room, I pick up Arthur's right hand, the one without the IV. This is the hand that grabbed the rope at the swimming hole in the summer and hurled snowballs in the winter. This is the hand that held that first cello bow, the one he bought at the auction. This is the hand that revved the Indian motorcycle, that changed the gears in his T-bird, that stroked his lovers. The hand is useless now, speckled with age spots, the fingernails long and gnarled. Bruises are blooming under the translucent surface of its skin, and I marvel at how any of us can be contained by something so thin, so fragile.

I am still holding Arthur's hand when Mom arrives and taps at the window. Her hair is still wet from her shower, and her eyes are red-rimmed and swollen. Standing beside her is a tall woman in a tailored pink suit. When I come out into the hall and take off my mask, she offers me her white-gloved hand to shake. She is old—although not as old as Arthur—and still beautiful. Her white hair is arranged in a loose bun on top of her head, and she is wearing dangly pearl earrings that match her necklace. When she smiles, I recognize her immediately. Coralee. Wife Number Two.

"I am so happy to meet you, Royce," she says, "although the circumstances are less than ideal." She glances at the still form on the bed.

"You're Coralee, right?" I say as I shake her hand. "I've seen your picture."

"I am indeed. And I have seen yours, although none of them do you justice. You have the Jenkins nose, you know."

I reach up and stroke my nose. "Yeah. Big."

She laughs. "I prefer 'patrician.' Now, I know these places insist on one visitor at a time, so why don't we let your mother have some time with Arthur? I could really do with a cup of tea."

I strip off the mask and gown and hold out my arm to Coralee. She hooks her hand around the crook in my elbow, like a southern belle at her first ball.

"Such beautiful manners," Coralee murmurs. "So rare these days." Mom snorts as she puts on a mask and gown.

When we get to the cafeteria, I steer Coralee to a table overlooking the garden. She lowers herself into the chair with a soft sigh.

"Black tea, dear. With a bit of lemon, if they have it," she says, "and perhaps something sweet to eat?"

I load up a tray with metal teapots, thick white mugs and a selection of desserts: a brownie, some carrot cake, a chocolate-chip cookie in a plastic package. What she doesn't want, I will eat. There is no lemon, so I add some honey and milk to the tray.

When I get back to the table, she is laughing at the bunnies gorging on some red-and-white-striped petunias. "Ordinarily I would want to shoo them away," she says. "They're destructive little beasts, but I loathe striped petunias, so I'm enjoying the show."

"Arthur used to watch them from his window," I say as I set a pot of tea and a mug in front of her. She peels off her gloves and puts them in her purse.

"I bet he was wishing he had a rifle," she says, reaching for the carrot cake. "He was a crack shot, you know."

"Arthur Jenkins, bunny-sniper," I say. Watching Coralee eat, I realize I haven't eaten yet today. "Is it okay if I have the brownie?" I ask.

She gestures with her fork. "Help yourself. Got to keep your strength up."

We eat in silence for a few minutes.

"Where's Aunt Marta?" I ask.

Coralee stops eating and puts her fork down beside her plate. "In Australia."

"You mean she's not coming?"

Coralee nods. "I am her proxy."

"You mean, like, her stand-in?"

She nods again. "Marta is…" She hesitates.

I complete the sentence for her. "A selfish bitch?"

Coralee sits up very straight and glares at me. "There's no call for that kind of language, young man."

I glare back. "Why isn't she here then? Why does Mom have to do everything? It's not like Marta can't afford to fly out here."

Coralee's glare disappears, and she slumps back in her chair. "Yes, she can afford it. But she's afraid."

"Of what? Flying?"

"Of Arthur."

"You're shittin' me."

The glare returns. "I most certainly am not. To her, Arthur is still a powerful person. Why do you think she moved so far away? Why did your mother settle in Lunenburg? Arthur has always been a force of nature. Often a destructive one. Especially to his children."

I nod. "Yeah, I know. I've heard the stories. But he's changed. You've seen him. Marta should get over herself. Suck it up. Mom has."

"You're right," she says. "But I'm afraid she won't. So you're stuck with me."

She lifts her mug in a toast. I lift mine, and we clink mugs over the crumbs of our desserts. "To Arthur," she says.

"To Arthur," I echo.

Coralee and I finish our tea and go back up to the ICU. Mom is in a huddle with some of the nurses. Coralee gowns up and goes into Arthur's cubicle, where she eases off her shoes, climbs up onto the bed and lies down next to him, her face next to his on the pillow, one arm over his chest. I can hear the soft murmur of her voice, but I can't make out the words. After about ten minutes she comes out, shoes in one hand, wiping tears away from her eyes.

"I think it's time for me to go, Royce," she says. "Can you call a cab? I'm sure your mother wants to stay here for a while."

"Go? You just got here. What's the rush?"

She pats my cheek. "You'll get tired of me soon enough. I need to rest. Traveling is hard on old ladies. I'm staying at Arthur's house, dear, but I have no idea where it is. My bags are in your mother's truck. Could you get them and come with me?"

"Sure." We say goodbye to Mom, and I call a cab from the hospital lobby before I get Coralee's suitcases from the truck. Three of them, each one big enough to smuggle a small child. I guess she's planning to stay awhile.

"I'm sorry I missed the gala," she says as we ride into town. "I hear Arthur was in fine form."

"Yeah. He was pretty stoked, I guess."

"Stoked?"

"Excited. Happy. Enjoying every minute."

She leans her head back and closes her eyes, and I can see how tired she is, how fragile. Wisps of hair are coming out of her bun and there are smudges under her eyes. She opens her eyes when the taxi stops outside Arthur's house, but she makes no move to get out of the car. It's as if all her energy has been used up in flying out here and getting to the hospital. Her hands shake as she digs in her purse for money to pay the cab driver, and I realize that her head is also shaking, or rather vibrating slightly. Either she's about to collapse or she has Parkinson's or both. I help her out of the car, and she stumbles slightly as we walk down the path to the front door. I get her into the house and help her into Arthur's chair. The drapes are still open and the view is, as always, spectacular. Ocean, sky, mountains. A line of fish boats heading back to Fisherman's Wharf.

"I'm sorry," she says.

"Why?"

"For being a burden."

I laugh. "You're kidding, right?"

She shakes her head. "I used to love traveling. Now it just reminds me that I'm an old lady."

"An old lady with a lot of suitcases." I grin at her so she'll know I'm joking. "I'm going to put some clean sheets on the guest-room bed. It's kinda small, but the mattress is okay, I think. You gonna be all right?"

She nods. "Lovely. I'll just sit here and soak up the panorama, dear. Imagine waking up to this every day. Heaven."

She's asleep by the time I finish changing the sheets, putting clean towels in the bathroom and humping her suitcases into the guest room. It's weird to see her in Arthur's chair, her head lolling to one side just the way his used to. Her neck will be sore if I don't wake her up, so I touch her shoulder gently and say her name. I half expect her to yell at me, demand coffee, tell me I'm an idiot, but all she says is "Thank you," as I help her to the guest room. She sits on the bed and bends over to pull off her shoes. Then she swings her legs up onto the bed and lies down with a huge sigh that is almost a groan. I pull a fleece blanket over her and leave the room.

While she sleeps, I make a grocery list. Milk, bread, butter, cheese. I put on a pot of coffee and make myself a *café* without the *lait*. I wash the dishes and wipe the counters. I dust the piano and tidy the desk. I text Dani and bring her up to date. When Coralee gets up, it's almost dinnertime and I have made a decision. We will order pizza and I will tell Coralee how I know that Arthur wants to die.

Sixteen

We sit at the kitchen table and share a large meat-lover's pizza with extra cheese. Coralee has a Diet Sprite and I have a regular Coke, which we pour into proper glasses, with ice. Mom always says, "Only hillbillies eat off cardboard and drink from cans," so I get out china plates for our pizza too. Coralee eats hers with a knife and fork, which I find pretty funny. She eats a lot for an old lady—almost half the pizza—and when she belches delicately into her paper napkin, she giggles afterward.

"Excuse me. I haven't had pop and pizza in years. I'd forgotten how good they are. Very naughty though. My doctor would not approve."

I put our dishes in the sink and sit down again at the table.

"What did you do after you and Arthur split up?" I ask.

"Arthur convinced me to go back to school. He told me I was an educator, not just a nanny. He paid for my education. I got my teaching certificate and worked for many years at schools for girls in Third World countries. Sometimes our teams had to build the schools first, before we could teach in them. I stopped teaching when I couldn't get travel insurance anymore. That was a very sad day. I was a headmistress at a private school in Toronto for a while after that, but it wasn't the same. Too much privilege. Too many stuffed shirts."

I must have looked surprised because she raises an eyebrow and says, "You thought I was a rich old society lady, didn't you? Soft hands, never worked a day in her life. Watercress sandwiches for lunch. Bridge on Thursday afternoons. Cocktails before dinner."

"N-no," I stutter, although she is right about the rich society-lady part. "I didn't think anything. Other than that you were—are—beautiful."

"Oh, you are definitely Arthur's grandson!" She balls up her napkin and tosses it at me. "He knew how to treat a woman."

"Still does," I say, remembering how courtly he was with Midge and Bettina, how he totally charmed Dani. "At least some women. He's not that nice to Mom. Or the nurses."

"He was a wonderful husband," she says. "Attentive, funny, romantic. So romantic."

"Then why did you get divorced?"

She frowns slightly. "I couldn't stand that he was away so much, and I was left at home. I thought I would be happier with a man who didn't travel, who came home for dinner every night. And I wanted a child of my own."

"Did you have a child?"

She shakes her head. "Sadly, no. But I had a wonderful career. And another husband, a good man who came home every night for dinner. But no children."

"What happened to him—your husband?"

"He died a few years ago. Heart attack."

"I'm sorry."

"Don't be. We had a lovely time together, and the end was quick."

"What was Marta's mother like? Did Arthur ever talk about her?"

"I never met Marta's mother, of course, but I don't think Arthur ever got over her death. It was very hard for him to see Marta for what she was—a child, an innocent. He always saw Lenci's face when he looked at Marta. He tried though, especially that first year, when he gave up touring, but they never really connected. And Marta never forgave him for his absence." She stops speaking and takes another sip from her glass.

"What about my mom's mother? Did you ever meet her?" I can't bring myself to call her my grandmother. She doesn't deserve it.

"Your mother's mother? Feh!" Coralee scowls and spits—really spits—into her palm. "That's what I think of that woman!"

"Wow. That bad?"

"Worse," she says. "Much worse. She ran off with a flute player half her age. Abandoned her child and then demanded spousal support payments. Arthur, the old fool, paid her. He was heartbroken."

"Where is she now?"

"Dead."

"Does Mom know?"

Coralee nods. "It was many years ago—a car accident—but I think it was hard on your mother...to have all hope extinguished."

"I guess."

"And what about you, Royce? How are you coping with all this?"

I shrug and stand up. I don't want to talk about how I'm coping, or how much my mother must be hurting or how messed up this all is.

"Can I show you something, Coralee?" I extend my hand to her and help her out of the chair. She nods and follows me downstairs to the garage.

When she sees the T-bird, she clasps her hands under her chin, as if I have just offered her a trip to Paris. "He certainly loves his cars, doesn't he?" she says as I open the passenger door for her and she lowers herself into the vinyl seat. I like it that she still speaks of him in the present tense.

"Do you have a driver's license, Coralee?" I ask.

"In my purse," she says. "At home I drive a beautiful old Karmann Ghia. Pumpkin orange. Had it for years. Your grandfather taught me to appreciate cars."

"Do you want to go for a ride?"

"I thought you'd never ask," she says.

I run upstairs and grab her purse and a couple of things from Arthur's desk. When I start the car, the gearshift feels cool in my hand and my shifting is smooth and noiseless as we exit the garage. We drive along the waterfront, the setting sun behind us. Coralee rolls the window down, and the smell of the ocean fills the car—kelp and salt and a whiff of sewage from the outfall off Clover Point.

"Is it supposed to smell like that?" Coralee asks, wrinkling her nose and rolling up the window.

"Not really," I say. "But they still pump raw sewage into the ocean around here."

"Disgusting," Coralee says.

We ride in silence until we get to Cattle Point, where I park, facing the ocean, and kill the engine. I know kids come here to party and the cops do regular sweeps, but it's still light and I don't have anything to hide. I'm just a kid taking an old lady for a drive.

"I used to bring Arthur here," I say. "He liked to drink coffee and yell at the sailboats. 'Come about, you bastards. Trim the jib! Hoist the spinnaker! You're luffing, you moron!' If there weren't any boats, he'd yell at the seagulls or people's dogs. Or at me."

Coralee laughs softly. "You sounded just like him then."

Two Japanese girls in skinny jeans and high heels stumble in front of us across the grassy area that borders the rocks. One of them talks on a pink cell phone while the other takes a tiny dog out of an enormous jewel-and-chain-encrusted bag. The dog stands on the grass, shivering, while the girl says something to it in Japanese. Eventually the dog squats and takes a tiny dump. The girl scoops him up, motions to her friend and they stagger toward the silver Beemer parked next to us.

Coralee rolls her window down and says something in Japanese, which I interpret as "Pick up your dog's shit!"

The girl with the dog looks terrified for an instant, but her friend yells something at us and flips Coralee off before they get in the car and drive off, music blaring.

"What did she say?" I ask.

Coralee shakes her head sadly. "Not everyone is as tolerant of old age as you are, Royce."

"I'm not always tolerant," I say. "I used to get pretty pissed with Arthur. He could be such an asshole. I thought about stealing the car, going back to Nova Scotia."

"But you didn't." Coralee pats my hand.

I shrug. "I started to like it here, I guess. I met Dani. I got used to Arthur. And I didn't want to spend years in prison for grand theft auto."

"Very sensible," Coralee murmurs.

I take a deep breath and say, "He asked me to kill him. Euthanize him."

Coralee inhales audibly, but says nothing.

"He left a note on his laptop. I deleted it, but I've got it memorized. Wanna hear it?"

Beside me, Coralee nods. I recite the note word for word and wait for her reaction.

"My poor Arthur," she says, her voice thick and slow. "How desperate he must have felt to write such a thing."

Her response is not what I expect. Or want. I want sympathy and righteous indignation. I want wrath. I want her to be on my side, whatever that means. I want compassion—for me as well as Arthur.

"Before the stroke, there were days I really wanted to do it," I say. "Put Valium in his *café au lait*. Not because he asked me to either. Because he was such an asshole and he made everybody miserable."

If I think I am going to shock her, I'm disappointed. She doesn't recoil in horror or even disagree.

"But you didn't," she says.

"Not then." I hesitate, then carry on. "I tried later, at the hospital. With a pillow."

She strokes my hand and says, "Oh, Royce. You poor boy. What a terrible burden for you, my dear. He put you in an impossible position, but you were the only one he trusted. You can still help him now."

"Fuck that," I say. I don't want to admit she may be right, but I can feel my anger seeping away like air out of a slit tire. "So what's next?"

"You tell your mother what the note said. We talk to Marta and decide what to do. Together."

"What about...you know...the pillow...?" My voice trails off. I don't think I can tell my mother what I did. Not now anyway.

Coralee pats my knee. "You'll know when the time is right."

I start the engine and drive to the hospital. It doesn't matter anymore if Mom sees me driving the 'bird, but I still park it as far away as I can from other cars. Arthur will freak if it gets scratched. That's when reality sets in. Arthur is never going to freak about anything, ever again. He's not going to get better; he's never going to hum or sing or tell me I'm a nincompoop. His life is over, but his body is stubborn. Just like him. I help Coralee out of the car, and we walk arm in arm up to ICU. The nurse tells us that Arthur's condition is unchanged. I wash and gown up while Coralee goes to find Mom.

I sit on the edge of the bed and look at Arthur. His hair is growing back and covers his head like dandelion fluff. His stubble is longer than I've ever seen it. I get two towels from the bathroom and drape one over his chest and one behind his head. His shaver is in my pocket, charged and ready to go. It's not as effective on his cranium as Kim's clippers, but it does the job. I have to be careful of all the tubes as I shave his face, and I can't get into all the nooks and crannies, but when I'm done he looks less like a homeless person and more like himself. One thing about Arthur—he was always himself. No apologies.

When Mom and Coralee come back, the first thing Mom says is, "Coralee told me about the note. Rolly, I'm so sorry. Why didn't you say something?"

"Like what, Mom? 'Your dad wants me to kill him'? I didn't think that would go over too well."

"You could have told me," she insists. "We would have worked it out."

"Well, I didn't, so let's move on." My anger surges back, and I know it's not fair to direct it at her, but I can't stop myself. "If you can tear yourself away from your new boyfriend."

Coralee has stepped out of the room. I can see her out of the corner of my eye talking to a nurse.

"That's not fair," Mom says. Her voice is steady, and I know she's trying not to lose it.

"Whatever. Are we going to pull the plug?"

"Don't be crude, Royce. I know you're upset, but it doesn't help."

"So let's have a family conference. You, me, Coralee, Marta. One conference call solves all."

"It's not that simple, Royce."

"But it is. He wants to die. He told me. We have to make that happen. Without holding a pillow over his face."

She leaves the room, tears streaming out from under her mask, and walks into Coralee's arms. I feel like a total shit, but I know I'm right. Arthur is gone. He has left the building. And he deserves better than this.

I head down to the cafeteria and eat some Black Forest cake. The icing has a crust on it and the cherries are mush. Even washed down with Coke it's revolting. By the time Mom comes to get me, I am asleep, slumped over the table.

"Time to go, Royce," she says, shaking my shoulder. "Everyone needs to get some sleep."

I wipe the drool off my face and follow her to the parking lot. She shows no surprise when I say, "I'll get the car," so I assume Coralee has told her about the T-bird.

We drive back to Arthur's in silence, Mom following us in her truck. I park the car in the garage and help Coralee up to her room. She moves slowly and clings to my arm as we climb the stairs.

"You gonna be okay?" I ask. "I mean, I can stay." As I make the offer, I realize that I don't know where I would sleep. No way am I going to sleep in Arthur's bed.

"I'll be fine," she says. "Your mother needs you."

"As if."

"Get some sleep, Royce. Things always look better after a good night's sleep."

I nod, but I don't believe her. Tomorrow is going to suck. The day after that will suck. Who knows how long the suckage will continue? For the rest of Arthur's life, that's for sure.

Mom and I drive home in silence. She doesn't even try to start a conversation, which is weird, since she's usually a big believer in talking things out. Sharing. She slams the door when she gets out of the truck and stomps into the house, where she listens to her messages (three are from Lars), makes some toast and tea and disappears into her room. I pull out my phone and discover five texts from Dani, each one pissier than the last. Why do girls take everything so personally? I text her back: *I am ok. A is not. Will call u soon.* It's all I can manage before I stagger downstairs and fall asleep, fully dressed.

Seventeen

The next day, Mom is gone by the time I wake up. She has left a note:

Gone to hospital with Coralee. Back after lunch to call Marta. Please be here.

No *Dear Rolly.*

No *Love, Mom.*

I try to eat some cereal, standing up at the sink. It tastes like soggy cardboard, and I think the milk is off. I dump the whole mess into the toilet and watch it swirl away. My stomach heaves a bit when I think about last night: the things I said to Mom.

I go back to bed and sleep until noon. Then I go for a bike ride, shower and watch reruns of *Law and Order.* Thank god for *Law and Order.* So reliable, so binary.

Right, wrong; good, bad; chaos, control. Sam Waterston's caterpillar eyebrows are oddly reassuring.

Mom and Coralee come home just before two. Which makes it seven in the morning in Sydney. Tomorrow morning, I think. Or have I got that backward? I can't believe that Mom doesn't want to inconvenience Marta by calling her in the middle of the night. Marta deserves to be called at two in the morning, but that's not how Mom rolls.

We sit around the kitchen table, the phone still in its cradle on the counter. Coralee is wearing a moss-green sweater that matches her eyes. Mom has on the same jeans and brown fleece she had on yesterday.

"How is he today?" I ask.

"The same," Mom says. "The doctors…" She makes a sound as if she is being strangled. Coralee reaches out and pats her hand. "The doctors don't expect him to improve. Too much damage."

"So he's a vegetable," I say.

"Don't say that," Mom yelps. "He's not a, not a… rutabaga."

My laugh comes out short and sharp, almost a bark. "A rutabaga, Mom? Where did that come from? What vegetable would he be? A carrot? A head of lettuce? A turnip?"

Her mouth twitches slightly, and when Coralee says, "He's an artichoke. Spiny on the outside, with a soft heart," we all crack up. It's not funny, but it kind of is. It's hard to explain.

When Mom picks up the phone, though, we settle down. No way Marta is going to think we're funny. When she answers, Mom puts the phone on Speaker and we get down to business. Fairly quickly, it becomes clear that Marta, who hasn't visited her father in fifteen years, doesn't believe that he wants to die. She thinks I made up the note because I can't be bothered looking after him anymore. She thinks we are taking advantage of a frail old man. Coralee finally picks up the phone, clicks it off Speaker and tells Marta to calm down. She never raises her voice, but I can tell that she is not going to let Marta get away with insulting me or my mother. She totally sounds like the nanny she once was, and everyone knows you don't mess with Mary Poppins.

"Royce is not a liar, Marta. Arthur trusted him to see that his wishes were carried out. I trust him. No, none of us has seen Arthur's will. He may have left everything to the SPCA, for all I know. The doctors are very clear. He can't breathe on his own, or swallow. He has stated his wishes, and we need to honor them, difficult though that may be. Yes, it was unorthodox, but why should that surprise you? Yes, I do think it's the right thing to do. All right then. Tell your sister."

She hands the phone back to Mom. I can hear Marta blubbering on the other end.

"Later tonight," Mom says to her. "He may not... go...right away, but we'll stay with him. I promise. I'll call you when it's over."

She hangs up, and Coralee puts her arms around her. They stand with their heads together for a few minutes, swaying slightly and snuffling.

Mom finally breaks away, swiping at her nose with the sleeve of her fleece.

"I'm sorry, Royce..."

"It's okay, Mom," I say. "Really. Can we go to the hospital now?"

She nods and goes over to the sink to wash her face. Coralee heads for the bathroom. I pick up the portable CD player, which is sitting on top of all the boxes that were in Arthur's hospital room.

"How did all this stuff get here?" I ask.

"Lars brought it," Mom says. "They needed the room. What's the CD player for?"

"Arthur likes to listen to old show tunes."

"What?"

"Old show tunes. He likes them. A couple of days ago, before the last stroke, he was humming. Didn't Lars tell you?"

"Lars?"

"Yeah, I ran into him and told him about the humming. He thought it was a good sign. I guess he was wrong." I don't tell her about the singing. I think it might break her heart.

At the hospital, Coralee and I sit with Arthur while Mom talks to the doctors and nurses and signs some legal papers. I plug in the CD player and put on the Rodgers and Hammerstein songs. Coralee hums along and strokes Arthur's cheek while Mary Martin washes a man right outta her hair. We leave the room when the nurses come in to unhook him from the machines. When we come back in, Arthur looks more like himself, without the wires and tubes, but his breathing sounds terrible, as if he is drowning. The nurses have warned us, but it's still a grotesque, not-quite-human sound. Mom and I position ourselves on each side of him, holding his hands. Coralee sits beside Mom and runs her hand up and down Arthur's leg. Neither of them speaks, but it seems weird not to. I keep wondering if he knows we're here, and if so, is he thinking, Why the hell don't they *say* something?

So I do. "Mom and I are here, Arthur. So is Coralee. I'm sorry it took us so long to figure things out. Don't be mad." I squeeze his hand as his chest rises and falls. The interval between his breaths is getting longer and longer, as the breaths themselves become shorter. It's all I can do not to shout, "Breathe, goddammit!" Even though I know what we're doing is right, it still seems wrong not to help him.

When I can't stand the gurgling, rasping sound any longer I say, "I took Coralee to Cattle Point yesterday in the T-bird. Hope that's okay. There weren't any sailboats to yell at, but a little dog took a dump in front of the car, and Coralee yelled at the owner. In Japanese."

"I didn't yell," Coralee says. "I never yell."

He gasps, as if shocked by her words, and the silence afterward makes me feel as if I too am suffocating. I stop talking and bow my head. His chest is still. We all lean forward, listening, holding our breath. Mom says, "I think he's—" But before she can finish her sentence, he snorts. Loudly. We all flinch. Mom reaches for my free hand across the bed. Her grip is painful. Arthur gulps for air a few more times. He sounds as if he's choking. I want to run out of the room, but Mom is holding on to me as if I am a boat and she is an anchor. Finally, it stops. He stops. We sit for a few minutes in silence, waiting. Nothing. I keep my head down as Coralee leaves the room. She brings back a nurse who moves me aside to take his pulse. I could have told her there is none. She writes something on the chart—the time of death, I assume—and leaves the room. I go around the bed to Mom and put my hand on her shoulder. She is holding Arthur's hand against her cheek, and her tears are running through his fingers. I wish I had cut his nails.

I put my arm around her. "It's okay, Mom." She nods.

We stay with Arthur for almost an hour, not really doing anything at all. I know that other cultures or religions follow some protocol after death—tearing garments, burning herbs, wailing—but us non-believers

just have to make it up as we go along. Coralee leaves to
call Marta, and when she returns we tuck Arthur's hands
under the blankets—they look so cold—and say goodbye.
Mom kisses him on the forehead, Coralee grazes his lips
with hers, and I stand at the foot of the bed and sing,
"*Happy trails to you, until we meet again.*" Coralee and
Mom join in. "*Happy trails to you, keep smilin' until then.
Who cares about the clouds when we're together? Just sing a
song and bring the sunny weather. Happy trails to you, till
we meet again.*" I have no idea where that comes from, or
how we all know the words—maybe our right brains are
helping our left brains—but at least it makes Mom and
Coralee laugh.

In the days following Arthur's death, all I do is sleep
and hang out with Mom and Coralee. I feel exhausted
and sore, as if I've just ridden my bike over the Rockies.
All my muscles ache, my chest feels heavy, my hands are
always cold, my tongue feels thick and unwieldy, like a
hunk of sausage. I wonder if I've picked up a bug at the
hospital, but Coralee says it's grief and that it will pass.
Mom calls the school and tells them I will be back soon.
They are sympathetic, but one of my teachers drops off
my homework anyway; it gathers dust in the living room.

It turns out there are lots of things to be done after
someone dies—boring, necessary things like ordering
death certificates and canceling life insurance and

applying for death benefits (there are benefits?), but the only thing Mom asks me to do is come with her to the funeral home to arrange Arthur's cremation. The funeral home is in a low, ugly modern building on a busy street. A Muzak version of "Wichita Lineman" is playing on the muted sound system in the green and tan lobby. A droopy fake orchid sits beside a brochure rack on a low wooden table. The lighting is so dim no real plant could survive. The man who greets us is short, balding and middle-aged. His plaid jacket strains over his belly, and his tie has what look like ketchup stains on it. Or maybe it's blood. He speaks in hushed tones, as if he's reading from a script, which he probably is. His name tag says *Orville Beatty*.

He takes Mom's hand in both of his. "I'm so sorry for your loss."

Mom nods and tugs her hand away. "Thank you. This is my son, Royce."

He nods at me and ushers us into a room where we sit around a table, and he asks questions which Mom answers in a monotone. I zone out a bit, so I'm startled when Mom and Orville stand up and leave the room. I get up and follow them into a gloomy subterranean chamber filled with coffins. Very gothic, except that "You Light Up My Life" is oozing out of hidden speakers. Creepy.

"I thought he was being cremated," I whisper. The room is very cold. Maybe there are dead bodies nearby.

"He is," Mom replies. "Apparently you still need to buy a coffin."

"Bizarre," I say. "Why?"

Orville gives me a sharp look, as if he has just realized I'm a teenager and therefore unpredictable. "It's the law," he says stiffly.

"That's enough, Royce," Mom says. "Help me choose, okay?"

"I'll leave you alone," Orville intones as he backs out of the room.

"Thanks, dude," I say.

Mom and I stand in the center of the room and gaze at the coffins. Or caskets, as Orville called them. Some are lined with white satin, some have ornate brass hardware, some are polished to a high gloss, some have little Dutch doors for viewing the remains. My favorite is made of unpolished wood, wide at the shoulders and narrow at the feet, like something you'd see in a Western.

I point it out to Mom. "Maybe Arthur would like the *Deadwood* model. Simple, elegant, timeless. Comes complete with cowboy boots, a ten-gallon hat and a six-shooter."

She giggles and puts a hand to her mouth. "Shhh…"

"Or how about this?" I say, pointing to a cardboard coffin on the floor. "The Ikea model. Sleek, modern, biodegradable. Easy to assemble. Requires no tools. Buy now and get two for the price of one. Your family will thank you."

"Stop it, Rolly," Mom says. "It's not funny."

She's still smiling, though, when she chooses the plainest wooden coffin in the room. "I know it makes sense to just get the cardboard one, but it seems so... undignified. Disrespectful."

I shrug. "This one's cool, Mom. Can we go now? This place is freaking me out."

"Me too," she says, "Just one more thing and then we can go. We have to choose an urn for the ashes."

"An urn? What's wrong with, like, a big margarine container? Or an ice-cream pail? We're just going to scatter the ashes, right? It's not like we're going to put them on the mantelpiece or set up a shrine."

"No, but—"

"So why spend money on an urn?"

"I don't know, Royce. Don't argue, okay?"

Turns out there are infinitely more urns than coffins: marble, wood, glass, metal or china formed into every conceivable shape and theme. Did the deceased have a hobby? Well, there's an urn for that. Seriously, you can put Uncle Bob's ashes in an urn shaped like a golf bag or the gas tank of a motorcycle. Aunt Betty might prefer the pink teapot urn or the brass praying hands. I want to get one shaped like a pair of motorcycle boots for Arthur (even though technically he didn't die with his boots on), but Mom vetoes that idea, and we settle instead on a plain cedar box. Orville mysteriously reappears as soon as we make our decision. Maybe the room is bugged, and he has been listening to us in the next room. Maybe he knows from experience how long people spend choosing coffins (sorry, caskets) and urns. I don't know what I'd been expecting—overstuffed couches, Mozart, maybe some complimentary coffee and cookies—but all Orville says when we're done is, "Will you be paying by debit or credit card?" followed by, "The cremains will be ready for pickup in a week."

Cremains?

Hey, Arthur, looks like you're going to be a portmanteau.

Eighteen

I go back to school a week after Arthur's death. I could stay away longer, but I don't see the point. I am sad, but not distraught or anything. Mom has Coralee and Lars to hang out with, so it isn't like I'm needed at home. Coralee is staying for the reading of the will. At some point there will be a small gathering of Arthur's local friends, after which the three of us will scatter the ashes at Cattle Point. I'm not much use when it comes to party planning, so I leave them to it. As long as there's food, I'll be happy.

Dani is waiting for me at the bike racks when I get to school on Monday morning. She's wearing a short plaid skirt and a tight striped orange T-shirt I haven't seen before. She looks hot, as usual.

"Hey," she says. "You ready for this?"

"Yeah," I mumble as I take off my helmet and lock up my bike. "It's...weird. Kinda surreal. Did I miss much around here?"

She shakes her head, and her hair falls across her face. I'm not sure, but it looks as if she's put in some high-lights. Or maybe it's just the way the light is catching it. "Nah. The usual. Break-ups. Break-downs. Nothing major. Everyone missed you though."

"They did?" My voice makes a humiliating squeak, like I'm thirteen again.

"Course they did," she says. "Dumb-ass." She turns and walks toward the school, her red courier bag slung across her body. I grab my pack and follow her into the school, feeling better than I have in days. All because she called me a dumb-ass.

The reality of how much I've missed and how hard I'm going to have to work sets in during my biology class. Ignoring the homework that had been delivered to my house wasn't the smartest move I've ever made, but the teachers seem prepared to cut me some slack. For now. Some kids avoid looking at me when we pass in the halls, but lots of girls, many of whom I've never seen before, come up to me and say, "I'm soooo sorry about your grandpa. Are you okay?" Most of them touch me too—usually on the arm. I smile bravely and say, "I'm good."

"How long you figure you're going to be able to play the dead-grandfather card?" Dani's friend Josh asks me after the last class of the day.

"Shut up, Josh," his girlfriend, Taylor, says. "That's so, like, insensitive."

"I'm just sayin'," Josh mutters. "No offense."

"None taken," I say. "I'm giving it, I don't know, maybe a month. Then it'll be getting old."

Josh gives me a fist bump (for a second I think he's going to hit me) and turns to Taylor and says, "See, he's cool with it." She looks at me for confirmation and I smile. I am the master of cool. And really, it's not as if I haven't already thought about it. It's the kind of thing Arthur would appreciate.

"Later, dude," Josh says. "We gotta bounce. Soccer practice."

"Later," I say.

When I get home, there is a note from Mom: she and Coralee are at the caterer, choosing food for the wake, or whatever we're calling it. As far as I know, a wake involves a lot of alcohol and maybe some wailing. I can do without the wailing part, but some alcohol might be good. I've invited Dani, and I know she's not averse to a drink or two. She's not into getting wasted, or anything, but if Arthur's wake isn't a good excuse to get buzzed, I don't know what is. With any luck, we'll be able to grab some food and a bottle of wine and hide out in my room for the duration. I make a mental note to wash my sheets.

Arthur's lawyer, Ms. Copeland, comes to our house for the reading of the will. I get to leave school early to attend, which is a bonus. The lawyer is about my mom's age, but way better dressed: she is wearing a form-fitting white jacket with a skinny knee-length black skirt. Red lipstick, red nail polish, high heels, very short spiky black hair. I can see why Arthur hired her.

After introductions are made and coffee offered, she sits on our lumpy couch and starts to read the will, which begins with a lot of legalese. I am mesmerized, not by the words, but by the shape of her upper lip (she has a pronounced cupid's bow) and the smidgen of black lace visible where her lapels meet. I am imagining what lies beneath the lace, when she speaks.

"First of all, Mr. Jenkins wanted me to point out the date this will was revised. He called me to the house in May to make certain amendments. He was completely lucid. Understood?"

She looks up at me, and I nod. She has my full attention, although I'm not sure what she's talking about. She clears her throat and starts to read.

"To my daughter, Marta Johnson, of Sydney, Australia, I leave my house in Provence and its contents.

"To my dear friend, Coralee Hunter, of Toronto, Canada, I leave my house in New York and its contents.

"To my daughter, Nina Peterson, I leave my house in Victoria, British Columbia. The contents of the house are also hers, with the exception of the following items, which are to be given to my grandson, Royce: the 1956 T-bird, the MacBook Air and all my photo albums. There is also a letter for Royce in my safe deposit box.

"The royalties from my recordings are to be split between my daughter, Nina Peterson, and her son, Royce. Royce's portion is to be placed in trust until he is twenty-one, or earlier for purposes of education or travel. His mother, Nina, is to be the executor of said trust.

"My Francesco Ruggieri cello is to be sold; the proceeds are to be used to establish a foundation in my name to maintain music programs in schools in rural areas. The foundation is to be managed by my daughters, Nina and Marta.

"To Kim Adams, I give one hundred thousand dollars, with the understanding that, as long as she remains in business, my grandson Royce will be given free haircuts.

"To Ben Wadsworth, I give one hundred thousand dollars, with the understanding that, as long as he remains in business, he will make suits for my grandson Royce.

"My stock portfolio is to be divided equally between my grandchildren and the foundation."

"Jesus," Mom whispers.

"Holy fuck," I say. For once, nobody calls me on my language.

"Ditto," says Coralee.

"Is all that clear?" says Ms. Copeland.

The three of us nod dumbly.

"Then I'll get probate started, shall I?" Ms. Copeland asks. "As you know, he made you the sole executor, Mrs. Peterson, so I'll be needing you to sign a few things over the next little while. But it's fairly straightforward. Should all be done in a few months."

"A few months," Mom echoes.

"Yes. Submit any bills for the upkeep of the house to me—Mr. Jenkins left a healthy retainer. He was very thoughtful. Always kept things in order."

"Yes," Mom says. "I guess he did." Except for the living will, I think.

She shows the lawyer out while Coralee and I sit and stare at each other. I can't get my head around it all, especially the part about the car. He left it to me months ago, right after I started driving him around in it. It made no sense. I didn't even think he liked me then. I know I didn't much like him. Was I going to have to spend the rest of my life feeling guilty? Or could I just put it all down to the dementia, forget about it and enjoy being—let's face it—rich? Or at least rich on paper.

Mom comes back into the room and sits down on the couch.

"He gave me the house, Royce. That beautiful house. And I wasn't even nice to him." Her eyes fill with tears, and she grabs a couch cushion and buries her face in it. Even in death, Arthur can make Mom cry.

"Nonsense, Nina," Coralee says. "You moved here. You and Royce looked after him. You have nothing to apologize for."

Mom moans something into her pillow that sounds like, "But I didn't love him. Not the way I should have." At least you didn't try to off him, I think.

Coralee gets up, yanks the pillow away from Mom and smoothes the damp hair away from her face. "You did what was right with as much grace as possible, Nina. Arthur was lucky to have you—both of you. He wasn't an easy man to love. Now, we're all going to be rich—shouldn't we raise a glass to our benefactor?"

Mom nods and gets up and goes to the kitchen. I can hear her getting glasses out of the cupboard, and I think I should help her, but I still can't move. I have an awesome car, a laptop, a trust fund and a bunch of old photo albums. Not to mention the free suits and haircuts. It's unreal.

"I meant what I said," Coralee says to me. "You have no reason to feel bad. That wasn't what Arthur wanted. He wanted you to enjoy yourself. Get an education. Go to Australia and get to know your cousins."

Mom comes in carrying three wineglasses, a corkscrew and a bottle of white wine, which she holds out to me. I open the bottle and pour the drinks. We stand and raise our glasses.

"To Arthur," Mom says, her voice and hands shaking.

"To Arthur," Coralee and I echo, clinking our glasses against Mom's.

And then I do something I never thought I'd do: I get wasted with an octogenarian. And my mom.

In the days before the wake, I help Mom and Coralee get Arthur's house ready for guests. I set up rented tables and chairs, and lug cases of wine and trays of wineglasses. I vacuum the floors, sweep the deck and scrub the kitchen while Mom and Coralee fuss with flowers and food. There is no agenda, no minister, no master of ceremonies. Mom may say a few words. She may not.

My main contribution to the event is a slide show that I set up on Arthur's—my—MacBook. I buy a cheap scanner with some of the money I earned in the summer and scan almost a hundred photos from Arthur's albums. Then I create a soundtrack, a mix of classical music, show tunes, the Pussycat Dolls and, of course, Louis Armstrong singing "It's a Wonderful World." Sometimes I wonder if I imagined Arthur croaking "skies of blue," but I know it happened. I like to think it meant something, that he was telling me he'd had a wonderful life, that he wanted me to enjoy my own "skies of blue," that he was ready to go. Maybe that's just wishful thinking. Maybe his last words were random and meaningless, but I prefer not to think that.

Coralee helps me identify some of the people in the pictures—friends, musicians, lovers, wives, children. She has an amazing memory for detail, often identifying a person first by an article of clothing—a fur hat, a Cardin coat, a pair of wing-tip shoes; or a place—Paris, New York, London, Toronto; or an object—a car, a fringed lamp, a red velvet chair.

Together we sift through the photos, picking out people, places or things of significance: Arthur and his long-dead siblings; Arthur playing his first cello; Arthur and Lenci in Prague; Arthur and Marta in Toronto, with Coralee in the background in a white nanny's uniform; Arthur and Mom in Paris at a sidewalk café; Arthur in a series of vehicles—the Indian motorcycle, a red MG TC, a silver Austin Healy, a black Jaguar Mark IX, the black T-Bird. What I can't get over is how happy he looks in most of the pictures: his smile is broad and confident; his eyes are fringed with laugh lines. I had looked at the albums before and never noticed how much he seemed to be enjoying himself.

"He looks like a different person." I point to a picture of Arthur on a teeter-totter with Marta. "I never met *that* guy."

Coralee gazes at the picture. "I took that. We were in Caracas, of all places. It was one of the few trips we took as a family. We were very happy. These pictures remind me of something I read once: 'The past is a foreign country.

They do things differently there.' I can hardly believe we were there, but here's the evidence."

"So what happened?"

"Nothing. Everything. Loss. Old age. After you hit puberty, it's just one thing after the other until the day you die. You have some good years in your twenties, after you've stopped embarrassing yourself constantly and before your back goes out and your knees start to creak. And those are just the physical things. They say as you get older, your essential nature is revealed. Sort of like a balsamic reduction of the soul."

"But not everybody ends up like Arthur. You're not like that."

"Like what?"

"Bitter. Mean. Angry."

"Thank you, dear. But I have my moments. Doesn't everyone? And wasn't he also generous and funny?"

"I guess," I mumble, remembering how often he pissed me off, how I resented cleaning up after him, how I coveted his car, how I wanted him to die, how his farts made me laugh, how good he looked in his tux.

"I'm sorry you never knew him when he was young," Coralee says.

"Yeah, me too." I scan a photo of Arthur in his tux, standing next to Fred Astaire at a party; they are surrounded by adoring women in elaborate ball gowns. And suddenly I realize I did know this Arthur, but only in fragments: smiling and laughing with a bevy of women at the gala just before he died, charming the reporter and the photographer at his house, meeting with his lawyer to make sure the people he cared about were taken care of, flirting with Kim, buying me a tux. Fragments of joy encrusted by years of pain and decay. A rotten oyster with a hidden pearl.

Nineteen

The wake is subdued, almost genteel. No wailing, gnashing of teeth or rending of garments. I dress up in my tux pants and a white shirt, and Dani and I circulate with trays of food and drinks, making small talk: Didn't he have a long illustrious life? Wasn't I proud to be his grandson? What was going to happen to the house? Apparently it's okay to talk real estate at a wake. Mom and Coralee meet and greet the guests, who exclaim over the view and suck back the free booze. One of the guests is Midge, the reporter who interviewed Arthur before he died. I tell her about transcribing his story onto the Mac and she puts her drink down and pulls me into a corner.

"You're saying you got his whole story—verbatim?"

I nod. "He was in the hospital, bored out of his skull. We'd look at photographs for a while, and then he'd talk while I typed. It seemed to take his mind off things. Like dying."

"You still have it?"

I nod again. She seems about to ask me another question—she is a reporter after all—then she thinks better of it, pulls a business card out of her purse and tucks it into my shirt pocket.

"Ever since I interviewed your grandfather, I've been thinking about writing a book about him. Now's not the time, but I'd love to talk to you and your mother about it."

"Sure," I say. "I saw your article. It was good. Didn't make him into too much of a saint."

"Well, we both know he wasn't that." She laughs and heads off to find another drink.

My slide show is a hit, although when the Pussycat Dolls song comes on the soundtrack, you can see people's heads come up, like dogs smelling an intruder. You have no idea, I think. If I decided to speak, what would I say? Arthur loved the Pussycat Dolls. He watched CNN all the time. He loved women and cars. He hated drafts. He never stopped mourning his brother and sister and first wife. He loved his family—even if he didn't show it—and chocolate ice cream. And *café au lait*. He wanted to die long before he did.

I carry my empty tray to the kitchen and sit down at the table, which is covered in platters of sweets: puff pastries, truffles, brownies, lemon bars.

"You okay?" Dani starts loading her empty tray with more sandwiches.

"Yeah, I'm good. Just needed a break."

She nods and leans down to kiss my cheek before she heads back out to the living room. Her lip gloss smells like ripe strawberries. "I'll cover for you," she says.

I stay in the kitchen until I hear my mom's voice. "I was going to talk a little bit about Arthur, but then I thought of something better, something that says more about my father than I ever could." There is a pause as she sits at the piano bench and uncovers the keys. "My father expressed himself best through his music—I guess I've inherited that from him. His old student and friend, Martin Sutherland, is going to help me out."

I stand in the doorway to the dining room and watch as Martin Sutherland comes into the room carrying Frankie—my grandfather's cello. I recognize Martin from the photo albums—he is the principal cellist of some big symphony orchestra in the States. He sits and tunes the cello, while my mother waits. When he is ready, she announces, "Debussy's Cello Sonata in D Minor."

It's not a long piece, but by the time they reach the last notes, almost everyone, including me, is sniffling. Mom looks at Martin and shrugs.

"Arthur would hate to see his send-off end on a sad note, don't you think?" she asks.

Martin nods and Coralee gets up to stand by the piano. The three of them launch into a spirited version of Gershwin's "They All Laughed." By the time they get to *"Ha! Ha! Ha! Who's got the last laugh now,"* most of the guests have dried their tears and joined in.

When all the guests have left, Mom sits down at the piano again. While Lars and Dani and I clean up, Coralee curls up in Arthur's big chair while Mom plays: "Begin the Beguine"; "Some Enchanted Evening"; "Climb Every Mountain"; "Cheek to Cheek"; "Shall We Dance?" Sometimes Coralee warbles along, but most of the time it's just Mom and the piano. "Arthur would have loved this," I say to Dani as she dries the wineglasses I have washed.

She stops drying and comes around to stand beside me at the sink. "No he wouldn't," she says. "Are you on crack? He'd say, 'What the hell's that goddamn racket? Get me some ice cream, boy, and turn on the TV.'" She giggles and puts her arms around my waist. As we sway together to "Let's Face the Music and Dance," I lift a soapy wineglass in a toast. "Here's to you, you old prick."

"That's more like it," says Dani.

Before Coralee goes back to Toronto, she helps us go through Arthur's things. His room is the worst— beautiful "bespoke" pinstriped suits with giant shoulder pads and nipped waists, ancient cracked two-tone Italian leather shoes, cashmere sweaters with frayed cuffs, unopened packages of black Jockey underpants, dozens of stained ties, a box of cufflinks, a drawer full of stock-piled drugs, a bag of quarters. I keep his new shoes, which fit me perfectly; his tux, which does not; and a set of ruby cufflinks. The rest goes into the garbage or to a consignment store, along with most of the furniture. Arthur's desk and chair go downstairs into what will be Mom's office. The piano goes into the living room to make room for our dining-room table and chairs. The old TV with the stick remote goes into my room. We have the carpets washed, and Lars paints every room except mine. I want to leave it alone for a while before I cover the dingy beige paint.

The day before Coralee leaves, we scatter the ashes. Mom has done a lot of research on the web as to the best way to dispose of ashes. It's illegal, so we can't just stand around the way they do in the movies, flinging handfuls of ash into the air. For one thing, we might get arrested. For another, human ash isn't soft and uniform, like baby powder or flour. It's gritty and kinda chunky. I know this because I stuck my hand into his ashes after we brought them home. I also put some ashes in a jam jar and hid it in my room. Just a toe's worth, I swear. Later Mom tells me that she has done the same thing, but on a slightly grander scale: she used a pickle jar. Anyway, if you don't want ashes up your nose and in your eyes, and you're near a large body of water, apparently the best thing to do is to put the ashes in a plastic bag, submerge the bag and open it under water. The ashes will disperse gently into the water as you say your fond farewells. At least, that's the general idea.

Mom double-bags Arthur's cremains in two plastic grocery bags, even though she thinks plastic grocery bags are evil. I point out that since we are basically polluting the ocean, using a couple of plastic bags hardly seems criminal by comparison. She glares at me and says, "Thanks for that. Makes me feel so much better."

We get to Cattle Point in the late afternoon. It's windy and cold and gray. No Japanese dog-walkers, no elderly couples on the benches, no kids making out in cars. So far so good. Mom has done reconnaissance and picked the ideal spot, somewhere the tides will whisk Arthur away into the channel. We pick our way over the rocks to the edge of the water, Coralee holding my arm. At the last minute, Mom seems a bit confused about the exact spot, but she finally points to a place where there is a bit of an eddy by the shore.

"There," she says. "You ready?"

I nod and kneel beside the water, the plastic bags in my hand.

"Make sure you get them under the water before you open them," Mom says.

"I know, Mom," I say. "You told me."

"Does anybody want to say anything?" Mom asks.

"Too bloody cold," Coralee says, her teeth chattering. Mom nods. "Go ahead, Royce."

My hands are numb, but I manage to submerge the bags in the freezing water and untie the knot. Nothing happens. I rustle the bags a bit under the water and suddenly all the ashes come out in a single gray blob, which sits just under the surface, unmoving. We all stare at it.

"It's looks like when you add flour to water to make gravy," Coralee finally says. "Just needs a bit of a stir, Royce."

"A bit of a stir?" I say. "What am I supposed to stir it with?"

We look around, but the shore is bare of sticks and there are no trees nearby. I roll up my sleeve and plunge my hand into the ball of ash, which clings to my skin, coating me with a fine, gritty film. I sweep my arm back and forth through the blob, but even when it's broken up a bit, the mass doesn't move away from the shore. It just sits, reproachfully, as Coralee flings some red tulips on top of it.

"Typical," Mom says. "Ornery until the end." We continue to stare at the blob, and just as I am about to point out that I have lost all sensation in my right arm and really need a shower, a small wave, probably from a passing boat, sweeps the blob and the flowers into the channel, where it begins to move out to sea, still remarkably intact.

"Goodbye, my love," Coralee says.

"Goodbye, Dad," says Mom.

"Later, dude," I say. "Gotta go. I'm freezing."

I run to the parking lot, the plastic bags dripping in my hand. I can't wait to get out of the wind. There is a garbage can beside the car, and I stop to dump the bags, figuring Mom isn't watching. Wrong again.

"Don't throw them away, Rolly," she yells from the shore. "I'll recycle them."

I pretend not to hear her, but I swear I can almost hear Arthur's raspy voice as I shove the bags deep into the garbage can: "What the hell are you doing, boy? It's too drafty in here. Get me a *café au lait*." I laugh and run back to help Coralee over the rocky ground.

The day I pass my road test and graduate from Learner to Novice, I take Dani out on a real date: flowers, dinner at the Marina restaurant, a movie of her choosing and a post-movie toast to Arthur at Cattle Point. Not enough to make me drunk, but enough to bring tears to my eyes. I tell Dani it's because I'm not used to drinking whiskey. In reply, she kisses me and whispers, "Sure, Rolly. Whatever you say." After that...well, let me put it this way: Arthur would have been proud of me.

When I get home from the date, I decide to finally read the letter Arthur left me. It's on top of my bookshelf next to my favorite picture of him, the one where he's on his Indian motorcycle. Coralee had it enlarged and framed for me before she left. She also gave me an antique print of an artichoke, with an inscription on the back: *Arthur Jenkins, circa 2010.* The letter's been gathering dust ever since the lawyer had it couriered over from the bank. Mom has asked about it a couple of times—she's more curious than I am, it seems—but she hasn't pushed it. Maybe she's upset that she didn't get a letter too. Not much I can do about that.

I'm not sure why I haven't opened it. No, that's not quite true. I'm afraid it'll be like one of those horror movies where a corpse reaches out from the grave and pulls the dim-witted but good-looking hero into hell. I'm afraid that Arthur has listed all my faults: my selfishness, my stupidity, my lack of musical talent, my inability to make a perfect *café au lait*, my lamentable virginity. I'm afraid he will say that his will, at least as far as I am concerned, was his final joke, that he never meant for me to have anything. That I don't deserve it. I'm afraid that I will believe him.

The envelope is plain, white, legal size. Nothing remarkable. Nothing to be afraid of. My name is printed on the front in shaky capital letters. The letter—actually it's more like a note or a memo—is written on lined yellow paper and dated the week before his first stroke. The handwriting is atrocious.

Dear Royce,
Take care of your mother.
Take care of the car. Always fill it with Premium.
See the world.
Get laid.
You did a good job. Thank you.
Arthur

I turn the letter over—there is nothing on the back. I read it again. The words are blurry. *You did a good job.* I put the letter back in its envelope and place it next to the photograph. For once, I'm happy to let Arthur have the last word.

Acknowledgments

Many thanks to my editor, Bob Tyrrell, as well as to the rest of Team Orca, particularly Andrew Wooldridge, Teresa Bubela, Dayle Sutherland and Kelly Laycock.

I benefited from the insight and experience of many patient friends, who read various incarnations of the manuscript and offered their impressions and suggestions. Sarah Gee, Leslie Buffam and Tabitha Gillman were early readers; Maggie de Vries, Kit Pearson, Monique Polak and Robin Stevenson weighed in later on; and Amanda Adams gave me valuable medical information. Sarah Mnatzaganian of Aitchison/Mnatzaganian Cellos in the UK graciously answered my questions about old cellos.

I would also like to thank my father, John Edgar Harvey, who died in 2008 at the age of ninety-five. He did not "go gentle into that good night," and thus provided the inspiration (but not the model) for Arthur.

SARAH N. HARVEY is an editor and the author of *Puppies on Board, The Lit Report, Bull's Eye, Plastic, The West Is Calling* and *Great Lakes & Rugged Ground*. She lives in Victoria, British Columbia. This book was inspired by her experience caring for her aged father.